I0747125

Praise for <u>*We Have Reached the End of Our Show*</u>

"*We Have Reached the End of Our Show* is a beautiful and heartrending journey toward an inevitable, but profoundly meaningful, conclusion. Gordon's debut burns with a fundamental truth: that lives, loves, and worlds all eventually end, likely sooner than we think—which only makes what we do along the way matter even more."

—Jason Pargin, NYT-bestselling author of
I'm Starting to Worry About This Black Box of Doom

"Ali Gordon has crafted a gorgeously intimate story that feels like a gentle walk through the poignance of true love, the whimsical nihilism of creativity, and the gift of certainty in an uncertain world. I fell deeply in love with the characters, and by the end of the tale, all I wanted was one more moment with each of them."

—Amy Vorpahl, professional DM, writer, producer, host,
gamer at *Nerdist, Geek and Sundry, Buzzfeed,* and *Dropout*

"Through the lens of Gordon's evocative storytelling, *We Have Reached the End of Our Show* is a beautifully stark reminder of everything we fight to live for—right to the very end."

—Kara Badalamenti, author of *Cursed Coven* and *Phantom*

WE HAVE REACHED THE END OF OUR SHOW
Ali Gordon
WILDLING PRESS

Copyright © 2025 by Ali Gordon

All rights reserved. No part of this book may be reproduced, distributed, or transmitted in any form, by any electronic or mechanical means, without permission in writing from the publisher, except in the case of brief quotations published in articles and reviews and certain other non-commercial uses permitted by copyright law.

ISBN: 978-1-957833-21-7
LCCN: 2025932620

Front cover art by Mart Lett
Designed by Michael Hardison
Production managed by Mary-Peyton Crook
Proofread by Grace Ball

Printed in the United States of America

Published by

www.wildlingpress.com

*To everyone who helped me through
the end of the world.*

TWENTY-FIVE DAYS

It starts like a rising dread, and then all at once, there's too much to make sense of. A roaring sound like a jet engine, followed by a hot, white light.

The hair on the back of Gabe's neck curls. His throat closes around acrid, scalding air. His eyes shake violently in their sockets. He knows he should feel terror, but he cannot feel anything at all. He tilts his head back toward a bright and empty sky fizzing like television static.

Gabe jerks awake, out of breath and with a metallic, sour taste in the back of his throat. He can see nothing. Above him, there is the vague aureole of a halogen bulb and fuzziness surrounding it. Blinking doesn't clear away the haze.

The pillow is soft but damp behind Gabe's flushed neck. Josie is humming in the kitchen.

"Jo," Gabe calls for him. "Can you c'mere?"

He hears Josie pad heavily in.

"Are you all right?" Josie asks. Gabe looks toward him in the doorway, but he's more a lack-of-light than any real discernable shape.

"I can't really see right now," Gabe says. He hears some frantic clattering, and then the bed dips under the weight of Josie beside him.

"You can't see anything?"

"No, I can see some. I can see your outline."

Something flits in front of Gabe's face. He can feel the movement of air over the bridge of his nose more than he can see what he assumes is Josie's hand.

"Can you see that?"

"A bit, yeah."

"Is everything dark?"

Gabe considers. "No. Everything is too light."

"Should I call Doctor Hach?"

Gabe has no interest in doing that, so he tries to swallow back his alarm at discovering a new symptom or side effect after a long, predictable stretch of the same ailments reliably materializing and ebbing away.

"Let's just see if it clears up," Gabe suggests.

Josie rustles around in the drawer of the nightstand before brusquely lifting Gabe's hand off the duvet. "Take these," Josie orders and shakes pills into Gabe's awaiting palm. "And this one too."

"What—"

Josie anticipates him and presses his finger gently over where each pill lies in his palm. "These two are for the seizures," he says, and then fingers a sharp, crescent half-pill. "And that's the sumatriptan in case this is a migraine."

Josie, too, anticipates the water, and Gabe finds a cool glass already at his lips. He gulps the medication down in one swallow and is guided gently back against his pillow.

"Thank you," Gabe rasps and watches the shape-of-Josie turn and immediately busy himself with something across the room. Gabe knows Josie well enough to know the behavior is odd.

As if on cue, Josie clears his throat. "Speaking of Doctor Hach," he begins, "he actually left a message, um, yesterday."

"Oh?" says Gabe.

"Do you remember a year or so ago, he mentioned some experimental treatment? He sounded hopeful about it."

"I don't."

"Well," Josie continues, and then as if turning the key in the engine once more, reemphasizes, "*Well*. He left a message."

"You said."

"And it sounds like they're doing a second round of testing, and a spot in this group has opened up for you."

Gabe's eyes still seem to be taking in more light than is necessary, but it is relenting a bit, and now he can see the very clear outline of Josie's apologetic, hunched shoulders, standing like a sentinel at the end of the bed.

"No," says Gabe.

"I know why you're saying that."

"Yes, I'm saying it because we *agreed*," Gabe retaliates, heaving himself upright in the bed. "Both of us agreed. I'm not going back into treatment."

"But, honey," Josie says, voice suddenly splintered and small. "What if this one works?"

Gabe's vision starts to equalize. Enough to see that fat, heavy tears have begun to roll down Josie's cheeks.

Josie is broad-faced and pragmatic and remarkably practiced at persevering through discomfort. Without instruction or suggestion, he slipped into the role of nurse with ease and never discharged himself from the position. He was just that sort—duty bound, pliant, dissolvable.

Gabe finds himself ravenous for the Josie of unruly emotions. For years, they discovered so much together that was so good; Gabe's desire to shepherd Josie into the delightful and unknown had always bordered on hedonistic. It's sick, and perhaps unkind, but it has been three long years since Gabe's cancer diagnosis and Josie's devolvement from boyfriend to caregiver, so Gabe finds even these brief moments of messiness in Josie's grief appealing.

"Baby," Gabe entreats, reaching out an arm. "C'mere."

Josie hiccups, scrubbing his palm over his face. "I'm so sorry."

"Please c'mere, please. You're so sweet to me."

"Stop," Josie protests but nonetheless alights on the edge of the bed, letting Gabe rest his arm around his waist. Josie looks down at him, forcing a watery smile, but cannot hide the bald misery in his expression.

"I know," Gabe says, which is not untrue or placating. He does know. "I'm not doing this to make you miserable."

"I know," Josie echoes. He does know.

"I like being able to eat your cooking. I went for a run on Saturday. You noticed that, right?"

"Yes."

"And, feel," Gabe says, guiding Josie's hand to the back of his head. He closes his palm around Josie's fingers, curling it into the hair at the nape of his neck.

"There's so much," says Josie.

"And *thick*! How long since my hair has felt—?"

"It feels so good." Josie sighs. "I know."

"Shouldn't I die with all this nice hair? Don't I deserve that?"

Gabe watches Josie swallow thickly. "Of course you do."

"I'll be so handsome in my casket," Gabe says and feels Josie winding a lock of hair around his finger. They both gasp at the very present delight and the sharp recollection of long-past intimacy. "Will you be able to stop the mourners from trying to leap inside?"

Josie blubbers a startled laugh, as if against his will. "Please stop."

"*Hubba, hubba,*" Gabe keens, contorting his face in mock anguish. "Poor hunk."

"Oh," Josie scolds, but he's flushed down to his neck. "Please stop. I don't want to think about it. I have to go to work."

Josie kisses the corner of Gabe's mouth, then stands and smooths his palms down the front of his rumpled khakis.

"How's your vision?"

"Can't complain about the view," answers Gabe.

Josie vaults expertly over the flirtation. "Call me if it doesn't improve," he instructs. "And you'll eat?"

"I'll eat."

Josie shuffles about for his bag and shoes and turns to wave goodbye.

"Don't be gone long," Gabe calls after him and only knows Josie is gone when he hears the front door click shut; his vision still doesn't extend far beyond his lap. Gabe exhales and fumbles for the television remote, talk show chatter the familiar backdrop of his days.

The news breaks in the late afternoon.

Gabe is awake and idly stretching on the floor of the bedroom, flat on his back with his right knee hugged to his chest. He flexes and unflexes a tight ankle as he contemplates the dusty light fixture above, his eyesight having equalized, but the daily scenery infuriatingly monotonous.

The woman's voice on the television pitches high with alarm as she says, "We're getting some . . . some breaking news. Um. Hold please."

And the studio around her goes completely silent.

Gabe rocks up the length of his spine until he is sitting. On the television, the camera lingers on an empty daytime talk show set and then cuts to commercials.

He reaches for the remote and flicks up through the numbers. Every broadcast tracks in a chillingly similar way: news stations linger on long, silent shots of huddles of people inside the studio. Live talk shows cut to looping music over *"Be back soon!"* cards. Loud commercials for body soap soldier cheerily onward but cut to black instead of returning to cooking shows.

Gabe's blood turns icy. He rushes to the window, but Manhattan seems eerily unperturbed. No fire, no smoke, no darkness, no plague. On the television, he catches the end of a sentence: ". . . every effort is being made to avoid this collision, which will—which *would* cause certain destruction—should the threat not be eliminated within twenty-five days."

Gabe is transfixed by the young reporter, an open-faced blonde woman with glassy eyes and a quivering lower lip, who still manages to read from a teleprompter with expertly practiced professionalism. The makeup under her eyes is dark and smudged, but her lipstick remains perfect and plum.

She's going to be sick, Gabe thinks and feels compelled to avert his eyes. Pity and disgust roil viciously inside of him in equal measure, so much so that he can no longer comprehend the words she's saying.

His phone rings on his nightstand.

"Jo," he answers without needing to see the caller ID. His tongue feels too big in his mouth. "What the fuck is happening?"

"I'm trying to get home," Josie shouts.

Gabe doesn't understand why he's shouting.

"Are you home? Are you safe?" Josie asks.

"I'm home," Gabe assures him. "Are you hurt?"

"I'm on my way—the trains . . . I can't get on any of the trains. I'm walking."

"Will you be all right?"

He hears Josie panting hard.

"Josie?" he says louder. "Will you be all right?"

"Someone dropped their bike," Josie says, his pitch rising hysterically. "I—I—I'm taking it. Gabe, I'm taking the bike."

"Go safely, baby," Gabe eases, trying to keep his voice steady. "Get home to me."

"I took their bike. I'm coming across the park. Oh my god, there are so many people."

The television has now begun broadcasting a news ticker that scrolls endlessly, the same text over and over:

THE UNITED STATES HAS DECLARED A STATE OF EMERGENCY. THE UNITED STATES HAS DECLARED A STATE OF EMERGENCY. THE UNITED STATES HAS DECLARED A STATE OF EMERGENCY.

"I'm going to hell," Josie keens.

"Don't go there," Gabe says. "Really, Josie, you can't start."

"I'm coming across the park," Josie repeats numbly. "Look at all these people. Look at all of these people, everywhere."

He barks a high, hysterical sound.

"Gabe, it's the end of the world."

◆◆◆

By the time Josie collapses through the front door, the state of emergency has been extended globally. Gabe has a clearer sense of the matter: Jupiter's gravitational influence has caused an asteroid to become dislodged from its orbit, now careening at twenty-two kilometers a second through space with Earth directly in its path. The velocity of impact would be catastrophic. *Unsurvivable*, though no one on the TV or radio says that word, exactly. There is a mantra that keeps being intoned hollowly, no matter the news presenter or the channel: "Though unprecedented, scientists are hopeful . . ."

"Gabe," Josie keeps repeating, frozen in the hallway. "Gabe. You've heard? Gabe. You know?"

Josie's whole body tremors violently. Gabe has to bend down and help him out of his shoes.

The role reversal is not lost on Gabe—frequently chemo-weakened, frequently invalid, frequently doted-upon and rarely fit to return the favor. Gabe realizes he may be alone in being able to process irony at the moment, with Josie so toppled by shock and exhaustion that he stands with both palms flat against the wall, as if he could be flung off his feet at any moment.

Gabe ushers him into their kitchen, and Josie falls back into a chair. It scrapes across the linoleum with a whine, which Josie echoes, a sick sound from deep in his gut.

"I'm so glad you're safe," Gabe says, and Josie reaches for his hand and grips it painfully hard.

"It was awful," Josie begins, his hysteria ballooning as he speaks. "I was in a session with a student when the principal came in and told me to follow him, because we had to collect the children. There were already parents in the lobby. All of them were shouting and I could see they were scared, but I didn't know what they were scared of yet." His words eke out between heaving breaths. "I didn't even know what was happening, and I was thinking about you alone here at home, and all the while I was imagining the worst, and it's still worse than that; it's still worse than the worst thing I imagined."

Gabe hushes him rhythmically, smoothing his hands over Josie's sloped shoulders.

"Am I supposed to go back tomorrow?" Josie asks, and though Gabe suspects Josie already knows the answer, he also suspects conversing is the only thing keeping Josie from diving headfirst into despair.

"No, baby."

"My sweater is in my office," Josie mourns. "And all those speech pathology workbooks. I've had them since college."

"Why don't we see what happens," Gabe placates. "They're looking for a solution. That's what everyone says on TV."

Josie's back suddenly tenses under Gabe's hand. Josie rises, swaying momentarily on unsteady legs. Gabe reaches to brace him, but he circles away, hands fisted into the front of his untucked, rumpled button-down.

"You don't believe that," Josie barks. It has the severe and certain tone of a threat. It's an uncommon shade on Josie, rigid and seething.

Gabe raises his palms in surrender almost reflexively. "No, Jo, I don't."

Josie slumps, the temper having torn through him like a brief, strong wind. "Twenty-five days, they said," he says, his head hung low, eyes covered by his sweat-mussed hair. "I heard it on the radio. That's not even a month, Gabe."

"Right."

"What are we going to do?" Josie ping-pongs restlessly from one end of the tiny kitchen to the other. "The city is going to get crazy. You could feel it already on the street. All the misery."

Gabe herds Josie into his arms. With Josie flush against him, the dome of his head just below Gabe's cheek, Gabe can feel Josie's heart hammering in his rib cage, smell the lingering adrenaline sweat and the tang of outdoors on his clothes.

"Gabe, I'm so scared," Josie whines against his throat. "What are we going to *do?*"

Poor Josie, Gabe thinks. *Poor, poor, Josie.*

"I think . . ." Gabe begins cautiously. "I mean, what is there to do except what we've already been doing?"

Josie shifts in Gabe's arms, looking up at him through wet eyelashes. "What does that mean?" he asks hoarsely.

"You and I will be together for the rest of the days we have left. And we'll do what we want. Just like we've been doing all this time."

"I don't know how you can be so calm," Josie says. The barb of accusation is apparent, if unintentional.

"I don't know either," Gabe answers. There had been panic at the start: the barrage of bad news, the palpable grief of the shell-shocked reporters, the impatience for Josie to return safely. But it had all sloughed off the longer Josie was home, until Gabe was feeling not just calm but peaceful. Sedated. "It was easy to be calm when I knew you needed help," Gabe says, but he knows it's something deeper than that. Something truer, and harder to name.

"I'm fine, Gabe," Josie rebuffs, both of his hands splayed over his own chest, as if that demonstrated some inarguable solidity. "Are *you?*"

Gabe swallows. Yes, he is. He's fine. It is not the correct answer. "I guess it's different if you already know." He manages a vague gesticulation toward himself.

"What?"

Gabe hesitates. Not because he doesn't know how to express it, but because he knows exactly how to put it into words.

"What," Josie says, no longer a question.

"Life won't be all that different for me," Gabe admits, "except . . ."

Gabe watches Josie carefully. His eyes flick to Josie's throat as he swallows, and then back up to his watchful, unquestioning eyes.

". . . I don't have to die before you," Gabe finishes, and Josie's face goes pink, and then very white, and he turns and vomits into the sink.

The warmth does feel nice, Josie thinks, and it is his first conscious thought since doubling over the sink in the kitchen. Gabe is running a wet washcloth over Josie's chin and mouth, which tastes of sour bile. The washcloth settles on the back of his clammy neck.

"Good?"

"Mm," Josie assents. There's a mug of cool water and two little orange pills pressed into his palm, which Josie takes unquestioningly. He'd been divested of his shirt and khakis at some point. He walks past them, still crumpled on the living room floor, as Gabe ushers him into the bedroom.

"You'll just lie down for a minute, right?" Gabe asks, pulling back the duvet.

Josie teeters into the bed uneasily. Talking seems beyond his abilities at the moment.

"That's it," says Gabe, helping Josie lie back against the pillow. Gabe clicks off the overhead light. "Just a minute. I'll be back soon."

Josie is left in the darkened bedroom. He doesn't know what time it is or, beyond that, why it even matters. Would it matter if he ever left this bed? No one was expecting him. No one ever would. He can hear Gabe scrubbing out the kitchen sink where Josie had been sick. He listens to only that for a while. It makes Josie terribly sad.

"Hello?" Gabe calls. Josie tries to find his voice to answer, but before he can swallow the stone in his throat, Gabe continues, "Yeah, of course it's a good time. Are you okay?"

The phone. Of course. Josie strains to hear anything in the silence that follows.

"Lisi, Lisi, Lisi," Josie hears Gabe chant sharply, as if calling someone back from a precipice. "Just breathe and talk to me."

There's rustling, and then her voice, tinny and small through the speakerphone. Josie catches just the end of her sentence,

". . . just don't fucking believe it. I can't believe, I mean, I don't think my brain is *literally* able to, to, to believe anything about it!"

"Yeah, we feel the same over here," Gabe answers. Josie feels odd being the silent half of that "we."

"Do you think the, um . . . The people are saying . . . Do you think they're right about scientists having some plan?"

A significant silence. Josie cannot see him, but can perfectly imagine Gabe's expression, reflective and still. Always considering his words.

"No, Lisi, I don't think so."

"Fuck," she hisses. "Oh, fuck, Gabe. I know you're right."

Gabe passes in front of the open door, looking mournfully down at the phone in his palm. The light illuminates him from below, casting eerie shadows that catch in the sharper angles of his face. Josie closes his eyes and pretends to be sleeping, afraid to get pulled into their conversation. He has nothing to offer.

"I just don't want it to be true!" Lisi wails.

"Are you going to be okay tonight?"

She plows over him, the question unheard and unanswered. That was her way, Josie thinks sourly.

"I tried to book a flight and at first I thought there was nothing available because everything was purchased, so I clicked through every date at every airport I could think of, but nothing. No flights out *of* anywhere *to* anywhere. And then I realized—it's not that people aren't trying to leave. It's who's gonna fly the airplanes, you know? Who's out there doing their job when there aren't jobs anymore?"

"Right," Gabe answers.

"So now I'm like, what the fuck do I do? Am I going to die in New York City? Am I never going to see my parents again?"

Gabe crosses again in front of the door, nodding his head and listening as Lisi's mania peters off into sobs.

"I'm sorry," she apologies, voice hoarse. "I didn't know who else to call."

"You can always call me," Gabe answers.

"You're the only person I know here," Lisi says, which makes Josie prickle with annoyance. Lisi appeared to have many friends, which she was exceedingly vocal about in her very visible, active presence on social media.

But nonetheless Gabe sounds very tender and very sad as he replies, "I know, Lisi."

Josie supposes there's no accounting for what family does to you molecularly, the bone-deep tether Gabe might feel.

"Do you think you can find a way here from Brooklyn?" Gabe offers.

"Yeah," she says, and Josie can hear her rustling about on the other end of the line. "I'll definitely find something."

"So I'll see you tomorrow, and we'll figure something out. Right?"

"Right," she echoes. She sniffs noisily. "Sorry, Gabe. I love you."

"I love you too," Gabe says, and ends the call.

With the specter of Lisi gone, Josie cracks his eyes open and watches Gabe through the open doorway. Gabe looks down at the darkened screen for a long, quiet moment. Then he rolls his shoulders, exhales, and pushes his phone into his pocket.

Gabe does look stronger, Josie notes. His shoulders have broadened, sinewy biceps rounding out his shirt sleeves. His sweatpants don't sit quite so low and loose around his hips. Even his eyes, which Josie had always found so round and lovely and dark, seem to fit better in their sockets.

And then Josie thinks, *What does it matter?*

After five months abstaining from treatment for his cancer, Gabe is now beginning to look the way he had when they first met, but there are still tumors in his brain that would eventually kill him. And now, they do not even have the luxury of time. It doesn't matter where they travel. It doesn't matter the pills they take or do not take. It doesn't matter how Gabe fits his shirts, or how much Josie loves him. It would all mean nothing in twenty-five days.

Gabe approaches quietly, squinting into the dim bedroom, seemingly unaware of being so closely and thoroughly observed. "You awake?"

"Yeah," Josie says, his voice weak.

"Your head?"

"Better," Josie answers. "The medicine helped."

"You should have some water," Gabe says, and turns to leave. Josie calls out to stop him, but Gabe is gone and back too quickly.

Josie finds sitting up in bed a monumental task, even with Gabe at his hip to bolster him.

"Go slowly," Gabe warns as he lifts the cup for Josie, but the round coolness of the water is intoxicating, and extinguishes an ache behind Josie's eyes. He gulps it all down ravenously, dripping some onto his lip and chin.

Gabe laughs. Josie begins to apologize but stills as Gabe leans forward and kisses the wetness into his lower lip. Josie shudders against him. It's good. It's very good. Josie feels perpetually shipwrecked against Gabe's cliff face, as though dizzy in a strange new land. Gabe hums and Josie feels it in the back of his skull.

"I'm sorry," Gabe says against the corner of Josie's mouth. "I can't help it. You're so sweet."

"Oh god," Josie gasps, his hands fisted in the back of Gabe's shirt. "I don't know what's going on."

"Let me take care of you. Can you let me do that? Can I take care of you for once?"

Gabe shuffles into the bed behind him, pulling Josie's back flush against his chest. Gabe's hands settle where they like: one atop Josie's chest, the other cupping a plump hip. They exhale in stereo.

"Is this good?"

"Yes," Josie answers. Josie thinks again about Gabe's strong shoulders. He turns his face and inhales where Gabe's neck meets his jaw.

"Jo," Gabe begins, low in Josie's ear, "are you hard?"

"My head is full," Josie groans. "I don't know what to feel. I'm embarrassed."

"Don't be," Gabe laughs. He kisses the back of his ear. "Please don't be."

It is nice to merely sit in silence, to feel held. Even the city seems to have gone quiet around them. Josie wonders if it will always be so easy to pretend like the world isn't ending. Gabe's diagnosis had felt like a catastrophe beyond measure. Josie recalls ducking into a bathroom stall during work hours to weep, or sitting sleepless as he eased Gabe through monumental, week-long bouts of panic, and then nausea, and then dread. And even that had somehow faded into the ambience of their daily life, one thread in the tapestry of their relationship. Everything was incomprehensible. Everything was manageable.

"You're so good to Lisi," Josie says.

Gabe peers at him down the bridge of his angular nose. He arches an eyebrow. "She's my cousin."

"No one has to be nice to their family."

"Yes," Gabe says, "but I love her."

Josie looks away and takes up fidgeting idly with the loose fabric gathered around Gabe's knees. He doesn't know what to say, and so resolves it's best not to say anything at all.

"She's going to want to leave the city. She wants to see her parents."

"Do you want to see yours?"

"No," Gabe says resolutely.

Josie feels a cool wave of relief extinguish an anxiety he wasn't even aware he was harboring.

"I think I want to get out of New York, though."

Josie cranes his neck to look up at Gabe. He had a way of appearing both expectant and entirely unreadable; an invitation to speak your mind with no assurance of what you'll meet when you arrive there. Josie found it terribly enigmatic when they first met, and envied that what you gleaned from Gabe was only what he purposefully chose to share. It was tiresome too, in moments like these, though Josie would never say as much.

"Why?" Josie asks.

Gabe gives a half-hearted shrug. Josie feels Gabe's heartbeat quicken in his chest.

"What's the point in dying here, of all places?" Gabe muses. "And I think the city is going to get . . . I mean, with the amount of people? I don't want to fight for food. I don't want to fight for anything."

"Where else would we go?"

"Anywhere," Gabe answers breezily, one finger tracing a graceful but aimless little trail in the air before them. "Nowhere. Wherever we'd like."

Josie wriggles out of his comfortable embrace and gapes back at him in bewilderment. "Why are you talking like that?" he challenges. "What are you trying to say?"

Gabe looks at the blanket. Gabe looks at his hands. Gabe looks at Josie with very keen, very dark eyes. "We could take Lisi to Sacramento."

"Why would we do that?" Josie counters. He gulps back the ugly resentment that claws at his esophagus, the repulsion at letting anyone into their bubble.

"It would be nice," says Gabe and, knowing it's not a good enough answer, he continues, ". . . well, it would be *new*."

"How is this the time for new?" Josie gapes.

"How is it not?"

Josie huffs and swings his open arms in a broad circle around them, as if to say, *Considering all this?* "How would we even get there?"

"Lisi will be able to get us a car," says Gabe. "She has money."

Josie fights the urge to roll his eyes at that. In the nearly six years that Josie has known Gabe—and so, has known Lisi—she had never been wise with money. It was the subject of many of her winding tales of tumult, told laughingly, never more than folly. Her parents seemed all too happy to replenish funds as necessary. Josie always thought it at least a little odd, because Lisi had never seemed particularly close to her parents, or, in turn, them particularly loving, but they were more than happy to fund her arts education, and her Brooklyn apartment, and whatever other unexpected expenses arose. It was more than Gabe could say for his own parents, who were very intentionally absent, materially and emotionally. Josie had once tried to intimate that perhaps Lisi's parents could extend some financial generosity, but the topic left Gabe icy and obstinate, so Josie quickly learned not to press the issue. Instead, Josie had spent the last few years in an eternal loop of the same conversation with insurance companies and doctors' offices and banks.

There was, at least, a small relief in knowing he would never need to pick up the phone to haggle again.

"She isn't very responsible," Josie counters.

"She's twenty-six," Gabe chuckles with an amicable shrug. "Who's responsible at that age?"

I was, Josie thinks sourly, but even as the thought occurs to him, he knows the comparison isn't a fair one. He felt, in turn, equally protective and resentful of his own circumstances.

"I won't force you," Gabe says. "It's your life too."

"But . . ." Josie leads, sensing the pressure of what Gabe has left unsaid.

"Yes. But."

Gabe inhales. Josie watches him weighing his words, turning over and inspecting each thought with intense, measured consideration. "I've spent so many hours thinking about ways to make the last of our life together good," Gabe says evenly. "I can't begin to tell you the amount of times I've wanted to grab you and just run away with you."

Josie reaches for his hand out of instinct. Gabe returns a reassuring squeeze.

"But I didn't want to be selfish," Gabe continues. "What would it do for us, really? Maybe we'd have fun. But ultimately, I would be dead. And then, what about you?"

"What about me?" Josie asks. His throat has gone dry again, his voice emerging high and tight like some ill-played wind instrument.

"You'd have no job to go back to. And what about this apartment? Who's paying rent? And with what money? I couldn't do that to you."

Josie usually has his rote protests, and he has become very adept at summoning the correct ones at the expected times. There is nothing now. Josie's tongue is stuck to the roof of his mouth. Gabe, undeterred, rises to his knees. Josie mirrors him unthinkingly, buoyed by Gabe's magnetic energy.

"But now," Gabe says with a smile Josie recognizes well and hasn't seen in a long time, an expression that teeters on the border between deviousness and delight, "*now*, you're not ever going back to work. I'm never seeing another doctor. What reason do we have not to go anywhere you've ever dreamed of?"

Josie is overcome by a dizzy, carbonated sort of sensation. His eyes prickle with unshed tears, but he is aware he is very assuredly not upset.

His head feels too heavy to keep upright, so he fumbles his way back to the pillows and collapses gratefully there. Gabe follows suit. They lie on their sides, facing each other like opposite ends of a parenthetical, bracketing nothing but the sheets between them. Gabe is still in all of his day clothes, Josie in nothing but his boxers. Something about it is funny, Josie notes, but he can't quite work out why.

"I've never seen California," Josie muses at length. "I'd like to see where you were born."

"Sacramento's not near the ocean, unfortunately."

"Doesn't matter," says Josie. "I've never been farther than Indiana."

"No," Gabe gasps, but seems to instantly regret it, watching Josie's face purple with embarrassment.

"You know my family didn't travel," Josie mutters, burying his cheek in the pillow.

"I did. I do," Gabe says. "And the two of us didn't get to, either. I'm sorry."

Josie feels a hot tear track down his temple and into the pillow.

"Let me make it up to you. Let me take you so fucking far beyond Indiana it'll make your head spin."

"I have to think about it."

"Of course," Gabe acquiesces. He stares intently at Josie from his adjacent pillow. Josie breathes him in for a long moment in silence. His long nose. His dark, dark eyes, revealing nothing, expecting nothing.

Josie says, "I've never seen the Grand Canyon."

Gabe's eyes are alight. *There it is again*, Josie thinks: the Gabe driven by delight, by desire to wring every last mote of understanding and excitement out of any experience. This Gabe hungrily sucked doubt out of the unknown like marrow from a bone, as if it were something nourishing and sustaining.

I have to tell you that I've never kissed a man before, Josie had said the first night they met, cheeks already cupped between Gabe's two very certain and dexterous hands. There had never been a moment when Josie hadn't wanted to kiss Gabe, and Gabe seemed to intuit that long before Josie had. He ushered Josie carefully and lovingly into the unknown that night, and he did again and again in the years after, with a remarkably attuned gauge of what Josie would say yes to. Josie wonders if Gabe always knew Josie would say yes to this wild cross-country venture too but resolves not to think too hard on that. The pillow is too soft, and his head too heavy, and Gabe's hand too warm on his hip.

Gabe rolls his spine, vertebrae by vertebrae, until he stands upright. His chest heaves with exhaustion. He looks directly into the warm yellow spotlight and raises his right hand—palm forward, as if in benediction—toward the darkness that shrouds a rapt crowd.

"We have reached the end of our show," he says, then pauses. He soaks up the quiet, a silence sharpened and attuned by attention and interest.

"Goodnight. See you when I see you."

Gabe does not take a curtain call, as is his tradition, finding his way off stage in the blackout. He stands in the wings to appreciate the applause, the house lights raising, the dam-burst of chattering people finally able to share their thoughts. Some music with an aggressive bass line is piped through the tinny speakers as the crowd shuffles out into the lobby.

He collects his water bottle and the shirt he shed somewhere around the midpoint of the show. He has friends impatiently waiting to receive him in the tiny dressing room, the lit vanity mirrors fogged up from the presence of too many warm bodies pumped full of adrenaline and liquor. A can of cheap red wine is pushed into Gabe's hand, along with a towel. He fields compliments and well-meant mockery in equal measure, until they pour out into the lobby of Dixon Place, still teeming with patrons.

Gabe loses his friends around the bar, all peeling off to flag down another drink or stumbling into another acquaintance from the small circle of performance artists that frequent lower Manhattan.

One man lingers by the front door, a white-knuckled grip around his rolled-up playbill. Messy straw-colored hair falls into his eyes as he scans the lounge furtively, eyes settling on nothing. He'll find a brief distraction—watching someone exit or head swinging toward a loud burst of laughter from the bar—but once the instant passes, he resumes idly contemplating the room.

He has the round, high-cheeked face of an aristocrat in a Rococo painting; pale, plump, and youthful. His free hand fiddles nervously with a loose fastening on his coat, spinning the wobbly button until flush against the corduroy, then letting it unwind.

He doesn't seem to have a drink or company and, although he's wearing his coat, makes no attempt to leave.

Despite a posture that begs not to be noticed, the man has found a way to stick out like a sore thumb. Gabe likes that. Gabe likes strangers. More accurately, he likes fans. He'd moved past being too embarrassed to admit that.

He leaves his cheap canned wine on the bar and finds his way over.

"Are you waiting for a friend?" Gabe asks, sidling up beside the man. There is a moment where the small man seems not to register that he's being spoken to and instead casts a look briefly over his shoulder. Finding no one there, he looks back, wide-eyed and caught, toward Gabe.

The cool draft from the door is refreshing. Gabe pushes his hair back off his sweaty brow and inhales deeply. "Oh, god, that feels nice," he appraises.

The man watches him intently, seemingly vacillating between shock and relief. He opens his mouth to speak, and then closes it again, merely nodding his agreement.

"Am I bothering you?" Gabe asks.

"No!" says the man. "I'm sorry. I don't think you know me."

"I didn't think I did. I'd remember you," Gabe answers, and revels a bit in the quickness of his reply. It is perhaps so debonair as to be lost on the man, who only looks back at Gabe expectantly, a bit like a person waiting to find out if they're in trouble. "What's your name?"

"Josie," the man says, extending his hand.

Gabe shakes it and says nothing of his very clammy palms. "Josie," Gabe repeats warmly. "And I'm Gabe."

Josie gestures vaguely toward the crumpled playbill still in his left hand. "Gabriel Fish," Josie says. "I know. I really . . . I loved the show. You're very good."

"Thank you, I appreciate that," says Gabe. "And don't worry, no one calls me Gabriel. That's just for the stage."

Josie giggles like ice stirred in a glass. "Well, no one calls me *Josiah*, but I don't go on stage," he rejoinders with the confident delivery of a good punch line. But in the following silence he withers and busies himself with his loose button once more.

"Do you see shows here often?" Gabe asks.

Josie looks a bit taken aback. "Here?" he squeaks, finding something on the ceiling to fixate on. "Um. No. First time."

Gabe watches Josie's pinched, thoughtful expression unfold into a toothy smile.

"But I chose a good night!"

Gabe knows Josie isn't trying to flatter him into submission, but he finds Josie instantly, irrepressibly magnetic and—as much as it hadn't been Gabe's intention when he approached—desirable. "Would you like to take a walk with me?" Gabe asks. "I know a few good places nearby for drinks."

Josie's jaw clamps shut with an audible *clack*. He stares back fixedly, studiously, seemingly prying for any sense of sarcasm, or an implication he does not understand. "What about your friends?" he asks.

Gabe swings around with exaggeration, still sloughing off his instincts to perform. "Where? Which friends?" It does wring a smile out of Josie, which he counts as a victory.

"You know," Josie insists, his chin jutting toward the bar.

"They didn't have to dance tonight, so they're already very drunk." Gabe lays his hand over his heart. "I am not. I have been forsaken."

Josie squints, not quite looking at Gabe or anyone in particular. His fist tightens around the playbill in his hand before sliding it into his coat pocket.

"Yes. Sure."

"Give me just one second," Gabe instructs, clapping Josie on the shoulder. "Don't go anywhere."

He darts off into the crowd, feeling Josie's gaze prickle the back of his neck as he winds his way back to the green room. Gabe reemerges with his bag and jacket and gestures for Josie to follow him. They step out into the frigid February air, so cold it momentarily takes their breath away.

"Oh, look!" Josie says with a laugh. He gestures toward Gabe's head. "You're steaming."

Gabe turns and looks at his cloudy reflection in the darkened window of a closed boutique. He can vaguely see the hot air curling off the top of his head, the sweat there rapidly cooling and making his skin feel tight and prickly.

"Still warm," says Gabe.

"You worked hard," Josie appraises, which strikes Gabe as a sweetly guileless thing to say about someone's performance.

Gabe maintains the juvenile habit of investing in one stylish wool coat for the entirety of the winter months, sweltering in it in October and finding it severely lacking after January. He turns and finds Josie pulling large knit mittens onto his hands that match his large knit hat.

Gabe is run through with the very hot and very present desire to throw his arm around Josie's shoulders, which he resolutely quashes.

Josie is at least a whole head shorter than Gabe is, which Gabe finds both endearing and attractive. But beyond that, there is a sense of familiarity Gabe cannot place, as if Josie was a good friend from long ago. Someone who suddenly reappeared all grown up and wiser but not without all the reassuring comforts of home.

Gabe points down the block to a familiar cocktail bar. It is slightly nicer fare than Gabe would choose among friends, but Josie's warm, timid interest sharpens Gabe's desire to impress. For a person who impresses professionally, there is an appeal in knowing you're playing to an amenable crowd.

They are led to a table in the back, warm with dim candles and dark wood. Josie sheds his heavy winter garb. Gabe slings his coat over the back of his chair. The world narrows to the width of their table; even the Friday night din recedes to static.

"Cold," Josie chirrups nervously, rubbing his palms together. Gabe confidently orders them both whatever drinks the waiter recommends, and when the drinks appear at the table, they are presented as sophisticatedly as Gabe had hoped.

"So, um," Josie says, his thumb tracing the rim of his glass. "Do you perform all the time? Is that a stupid thing to ask?"

"It isn't," Gabe quickly reassures him. It entices a pleased little smile out of Josie. "Not all the time. I teach dance, for money. I'll dance in someone else's thing, if they ask me, while I'm choreographing and rehearsing my own shows. Which can take months. It's a little lonely, you feel stupid, you give up on it for a while, you wake up with a new idea, you take it to a rehearsal room and feel like the greatest genius who ever lived."

Gabe pauses for his self-effacing joke to land, but Josie only nods back intently. "But once I've got something in my body and the show is up and running, yeah, I try and perform it around as much as I can."

"Around New York?"

"I'm taking that new piece around the city first. But it would be nice to do a few festivals. There are some international ones I'd like to break into."

Josie stares at him, plump cheek fitted neatly into his palm. "You must see a lot," he says.

"Of dance?"

"Of art," Josie amends.

"I do see a lot." Gabe considers, then adds with a waggish smile, "Not all of it good. What about you?"

"Me?" asks Josie, almost guiltily.

"You ended up at my hole in the wall on a Friday night in Manhattan. You obviously see stuff."

"Oh. You know. Yes. And no," Josie says. He noisily sucks down the last dregs of his drink. "School keeps me busy."

Gabe cocks an eyebrow, inviting Josie to continue.

"I'm getting my masters."

"You're kidding. In what?"

"Speech language pathology," he answers, but it tips upward like a question. Gabe nods his understanding to encourage him. "I'm a few months from completion."

"Well, that's something to celebrate," Gabe crows, gesturing grandly for a second round of drinks to be delivered. "When did you know you wanted to do that?"

"I don't know," Josie answers and seems genuinely not to have an answer. He twists up his lips in thought. "I really can't remember. It was something an academic advisor mentioned. I knew I wanted to work with children."

"Do you?"

"I'd like to, if I graduate."

"*When*," Gabe corrects, which instantly flushes Josie pink out to his ears.

Josie takes another long and grateful sip from his replenished drink as a reprieve from Gabe's unwavering attention. "And you?" he asks once he comes up for air. "How long have you been into, uh . . ."

"Highly conceptual multimedia-slash-dance works about famous depictions of masculinity?"

Josie makes a vaguely assenting gesture with his free hand.

"It all coalesced in the last few years. But I've been dancing since I was a teenager. Maybe fourteen?"

"That's amazing," Josie says. "I feel like, you know, when I hear about great dancers, they've been doing it since they were really young."

"Well, that's because I'm not really a great dancer."

"That's not true," Josie says sharply.

Gabe is surprised by the conviction. It's flattering, and Gabe won't deny a susceptibility to flattery. "I mean, comparatively to people who are *daaahncers*," Gabe delineates, lowering his voice to a warbly baritone for effect. "Dancers first and foremost. I don't have that kind of technique. I do think you have to hammer that in early. I think it is an age thing."

"I didn't notice," Josie insists, quite forcefully. "I thought you were wonderful."

"That's sweet of you to say," says Gabe. "I mean that. You're sweet."

"Thank you," Josie demurs, his intensity fizzling away, returning to his familiar diffident habit of tracing the condensation on his glass.

"How long have *you* been interested in highly conceptual multimedia-slash-dance works?"

"Hm?" says Josie, lifting his head. "I'm not."

"You ended up at my show. So you're either interested in the avant-garde downtown dance scene, or you're gay. But it's almost always both."

"Oh?" says Josie with a feigned nonchalance as flimsy as tissue paper. His face has gone very red.

"Oh?" Gabe repeats.

For a moment, no one speaks.

"I wasn't trying to assume . . ." Gabe starts. Any suaveness he'd mustered had been a byproduct of feeling wanted and attractive, but Gabe always felt warmed and vaguely post-orgasmic after a good show, and it was very possible he'd twisted Josie's casual compliments into something more.

"No, that's okay," Josie asserts.

Gabe places his hand over his heart solemnly. "Josie. What I just did was very rude."

"I don't mind! I don't."

"I just can't imagine who else would be interested in seeing my work!"

"Well," Josie exhales. "I can imagine a lot of people would be interested in seeing you."

Josie averts his eyes and sucks down the last of his drink noisily through a straw. Gabe is embarrassed, perhaps doubly because of the insistence he shouldn't be.

"I am gay," Josie says. "So."

Gabe nods, relieved but wary of saying much else. He figures the next faux pas gets you, deservedly, slapped.

"I, um," Josie begins, then gets caught up in a roiling laugh that balloons until he is too hysterical to talk. Gabe only watches, completely unsure whether to feel relief or further mortification. "I've never seen a dance show in my life," Josie says once he regains the ability to speak. "I googled . . ." He wipes his eyes, his mouth. He tries to regain composure. "I googled, *hah*, gay events, plus Manhattan."

"And *I* came up?" Gabe marvels.

"Second result. And I really didn't want to see a musical comedy cabaret."

The curtness of that from Josie makes Gabe laugh. Finally, the absurdity of it has enveloped them both, and they spend long minutes trying to suppress their giggling, trying to decide who should speak first, and then realizing there's not much else to say before devolving into hysteria again.

The presence of a hovering waiter is what eventually cows them into better behavior. Josie dabs his cheeks dry, but bits of the white paper napkin stick to his reddened cheeks.

"Aha," says Gabe.

"What?"

"Your face," he says. He pats his own cheeks to demonstrate. "The napkin—"

"Oh, is it very bad?"

It nearly spins Gabe into laughter again, but he manages to stop himself, watching Josie scrub at it ineffectually. "Do you mind if I—?"

"Please," Josie says, and faster than either of them can comprehend the consequences of that invitation, Gabe is hovering over Josie's seat. Gabe places his right hand atop Josie's cheek and the other at the back of Josie's neck. Josie's gaze flicks from Gabe's mouth to his eyes, something wild and wanting in his huge black pupils. Gabe can feel Josie's desire palpably, as if it pulsated out of the base of his skull and into Gabe's open palm. It makes Gabe's stomach hurt to be so wanted and so wanting all at once, both idol and enthusiast. Gabe has to remind himself to step back, his work now finished.

"Better," Gabe says. "I may have missed some. The lighting in here leaves something to be desired."

"Maybe it's better outside," says Josie, who quickly blushes as though belatedly realizing the foolishness of that suggestion. But Gabe already has cash on the table, insisting it has been his treat, and Josie is following him out into the cold air again.

It must be late, thinks Gabe. Even the weekend crowds have begun to dissipate, or perhaps the frigid night has swept them inside. The street is empty and hushed around them. Josie hovers close at Gabe's heels.

Gabe turns to him slowly, appreciating how expectant Josie seems, so utterly free of pretense. So he takes Josie's cheeks in both of his hands.

"Oh," says Josie. His eyes squeeze closed. Gabe cannot help but notice the lightness of his yellow eyelashes, the strange fragility of them against his ruddy cheek. "Oh, um."

Gabe pulls back. "Is this not good?"

"Gabe," Josie says, then swallows thickly. "I have to tell you I've never kissed a man before."

Gabe enjoys the severity of his wording. *I have to tell you*, like the start of a letter from a heroine in a Jane Austen novel. But Josie says nothing else, looking a bit stricken and a bit ashamed, so Gabe tamps down his amusement and answers, "If you're wondering if that matters to me, it does not."

Josie nods and softens minutely.

"Does it matter to you?"

"Um," says Josie, as Gabe brushes his thumb past the underside of Josie's ear. Josie whimpers, his hazy focus settling on Gabe's lower lip. Gabe feels as if he is watching Josie untether into two: one Josie standing on two solid feet on the corner of Broome and Chrystie Street, and the other Josie dizzily gulping down the thin ozone above mountains.

"I don't mind," Josie manages.

"Is it something you'd like to do tonight?"

Josie shrugs, too discomposed for clever thought.

"I'm sorry," Gabe says, chuckling. "I have already notably fucked up once tonight. I really need to hear you say yes."

Josie laughs and sucks in an icy, invigorating breath. "Yes," he says and exhales warm into Gabe's mouth.

TWENTY-FOUR DAYS

Lisi arrives in a whirlwind, out of breath and already tearful. "Someone smashed in the windows of the bodega on your corner," she announces, dropping her backpack on the floor with a thud.

"What?"

"The bodega on your corner? It's absolutely busted up. All the windows."

"That's terrible," says Josie. "I hope everyone is all right."

"It's starting!" Lisi says, throwing her hands in the air. She slouches over to the couch and collapses onto it in a tangle of limbs and black denim.

Gabe approaches and sits at her hip. "Hi, chickadee," he says with a wry, gloomy smile.

Lisi instantly launches herself into his arms, clasping him tight around the neck. "You look really good!" she warbles into his shoulder.

"Yeah, how about all this hair?"

Lisi only holds him and trembles.

Lisi and Gabe have much in common. Both are very tall, with long limbs and large hands that might seem awkward or gawkish on someone less poised. They share a similar lyrical lower register to their voices, and thick black hair, which Lisi had always worn long with very stylish cropped bangs. She and Gabe share a penchant for dressing well, which was yet another way Josie felt estranged in their joint presence—always feeling egregiously short, plump, and pedestrian. Josie doesn't know if the genetics run as strongly in the rest of Gabe's family, but at some angles, she and Gabe could be twins.

"Um, some coffee," Josie interrupts as gently as he can, passing down a mug. "If you want."

"Thank you, Josie," Lisi says, taking it in her quavering hands. "You're so nice."

Josie reels with barely concealed surprise. "Sure, Lisi," he answers stiffly, watching her dab at her damp cheeks. He cannot recount another time she'd ever been so unequivocally nice to him. End times, indeed.

She takes a long drink and exhales gratefully. Josie has rarely seen Lisi so rumpled and barefaced. It suits her, as all drama and strife seem to, every expression worn expertly. Gabe had spoken about her talent as an actor; it was even more captivating in the technicolor of real life.

"I hitchhiked across the bridge," Lisi says, slotting the half-empty mug between her knees. "There are so many people leaving."

"Traffic?" Josie asks.

Lisi nods exaggeratedly. "Oh yeah," she affirms, wide-eyed at merely the recollection. "I mean, not everywhere. I woke up this morning and my neighborhood was so normal I almost felt sick, you know? Nothing seemed any different. Like, did I miss something? But as I got closer to the bridge, the *energy* in the air changed. Do you know what I mean? I could feel everyone's nerves."

Josie had been on the street as the news spread. He very much knew what Lisi meant.

"The Williamsburg Bridge was gridlocked. I asked someone about the Brooklyn Bridge, and they said they'd tried it earlier, and it was the same. So I just started walking, and eventually some guys picked me up about halfway across and dropped me off along the West Side Highway, and I kept walking up to you."

"Some guys?" Gabe presses.

Lisi shrugs. "Yeah, just some guys. They were going to the Holland Tunnel on their way out of New York."

"Please don't get into cars with *some guys*," says Gabe.

Lisi titters uncomfortably, shifting away from Gabe on the couch. "It was fine, Gabe," she says. "They weren't interested in me. They were interested in getting out of here."

She and Gabe stare each other down, the tearful, saccharine reunion shifting.

"It's not pretty," Lisi says. "And it's only the first day."

She seems nauseated by her own vatic pronouncements. Lisi raises her hands, shaking them out at the wrist like one might dry them. She exhales sharply through her nose once, and then opens her eyes. The morose moment resolutely cast aside, she takes Gabe's hand in both of hers. She looks momentarily toward Josie, and there's something apprehensive in her drawn, downturned expression. Josie's heart plummets into his stomach.

"My parents want me to come home," Lisi says, nearly a whisper. "They . . . well, you're invited."

"Mm," Gabe hums.

"They said they'd pay for our tickets. Both of us. Like I said yesterday, I don't think that'll be possible, but they offered it. And they wanted me to tell you that."

"I wouldn't go anywhere without Josie," says Gabe.

"Oh, I know!" Lisi squawks, her face purpling. She glances up at Josie again, then away just as quickly. "Of course I know that. I wasn't . . . well, it's not like we're flying anywhere anyway!" She peters off into a quick, uncomfortable laugh. "And, Josie, I'm sure you want to see your family too."

"I do not," Josie answers bluntly. He begins to pace in the hopes that it will distract him from saying something he'll regret.

"So, is this it?" Lisi asks, and then perhaps realizing the morbidity of that phrasing quickly amends, "I mean, are you going to stay here through the, um . . . through the end?"

Gabe searches for Josie's eyes. Josie nods back.

"What if we drove to Sacramento?" Gabe asks.

Josie sees the question hit Lisi like a dart. She recoils, her hands flying out of her lap like startled birds. One lands over her heart with a hollow clap, the other braces flat against the couch cushion. "Who?" she asks.

"The three of us," says Gabe. "We don't have to rush. We can leave when we want, travel at our own pace, see anything we want to see. And we'll get you to your parents."

The hand against Lisi's chest flits nervously—childishly—into her hair, tugging at a fistful just behind her right ear. "You mean that?" she asks, her voice shaking.

"I think it would be a nice way to spend the last days."

"Thank you, Gabe," she warbles, bubbling over with tears.

"Don't thank me," Gabe says. "It was Josie's idea."

Josie's head snaps up, his eyebrows raised so high they've disappeared into his hair. Gabe half-shrugs back at him unapologetically.

"Josie, thank you," Lisi effuses in one great, breathless gust. "You have no idea . . . I was so scared to go alone! I was talking to Mom and Dad last night and they're just, like, convinced I wouldn't make it." Lisi wipes the back of her hand over her wet eyes. She manages a sour little laugh. "You know them, they don't trust me with anything."

"I don't think any of us should be alone," Josie answers. "They're right to worry."

"I mean, I'm not dumb," she defends, "I was going to figure *something* out."

Josie is wise enough not to argue that. Despite his opinion of her, the idea of Lisi driving west entirely alone turns his stomach. He imagines her weary, hungry, the scope of the world tightening around her. It wasn't fair for anyone to see the end that way.

"Josie and I were talking this morning about how we think we can manage the trip."

"Gabey baby, we're in luck," Lisi crows. "Because I know where I can buy a car."

"Are you sure?"

"Trust me. I'll just give them cash. Who doesn't want cash right now?"

"We thought you'd say that," Josie mumbles flatly, to no one in particular. There would come a time soon when a handful of cash would amount to very little, but he strives to be grateful for it while he can.

"I'll call you when I've got it," she says. She rises to her feet, hauling Gabe up after her. With a purpose and the promise of company, Lisi seems renewed. Almost untroubled. "Thank you," she says, squeezing Gabe's shoulder. "Seriously, I'm gonna figure this out right away. We could leave tomorrow!"

"No," Josie interrupts. "Not tomorrow. I have to go to the pharmacy and find a way to get Gabe's pills."

Gabe's quick laugh is squashed under the weight of Josie's very stern look.

"No, you don't," Gabe says with an evasive waggle of his fingers.

"It's the middle of the month, so you're running low."

"Right," Gabe says measuredly. "*But.*"

"We're not leaving New York without your medication," Josie answers. "That's not up for debate."

"It's fine!" Lisi cuts in quickly, her hands raised as if she were a child caught somewhere they shouldn't be. "It doesn't have to be tomorrow! Two days is fine! Three!"

"We'll figure it out," Gabe says. "Just call me."

She throws herself into Gabe's arms and squeezes him so tightly that Josie can see them both tremble with the exertion. Josie has always known that Gabe loved her. The details of Gabe's upbringing were purposefully hazy in his retellings, but Lisi was always a deftly drawn character. She was all at once his mentee and confidante and co-conspirator in art and mischief. Josie had a harder time swallowing that Lisi's adoration might be similarly mutual, extending far past mere idolatry.

She hugs Josie too as she leaves, with less fervor. Josie feels the cold spear of revelation run them both through as they separate: they would be together at the end of their lives. Very little else seemed more important.

"I really can't believe you're here," Lisi says.

"You invited me!" Gabe protests, breathless from an exhale of incredulous laughter.

"Right, but you came," says Lisi. "That's wild."

"To your first show in New York? Isn't that important?"

The answer is yes, of course it is very important to Lisi, who had sunk hours into booking a theater, and coordinating rehearsal schedules, and printing programs, and emailing out invitations to everyone in her contact book. She'd checked off the RSVPs of friends and fellow classmates and former NYU professors, but it wasn't until Gabe had texted ten minutes before curtain, "grabbed a seat in the back row!" that Lisi began to feel like something unclothed and ugly could be exposed in the culmination of all that busywork.

Now she stands too close to Gabe in the overcrowded, overloud vestibule, still in her show blacks, sweaty from exertion, and too embarrassed to introduce him to any of her castmates. She resolutely avoids anyone else's gaze, afraid of any demand for her attention, anything that could pull her away and give Gabe an opportunity to duck out.

"You seem preoccupied," Gabe says.

"Do I?" Lisi chirrups, frazzled. "I'm not!"

"Listen, chickadee," he says, swooping down to kiss her cheekbone. "I can tell you want to hang with your adoring fans. I love you."

He tips his chin in an elegant little salute and turns for the door.

"Wait," Lisi calls after him, unthinkingly reaching for the strap of his bag to halt him. He stumbles, swinging back to find Lisi still connected. Lisi recoils, caught, immediately abashed. Her hand snaps back as if burned. "Sorry! Can I . . . Can I ask you what you thought?"

The instant those words have escaped her, Lisi is thirteen again, performing on the stage of a quiet Sacramento cul-de-sac, insisting on Gabe's feedback—real criticism—*Gabe, I can handle it*—on every piece of poetry and every dramatic monologue recited for her favorite audience of one.

Gabe exhales, warm and benevolent. "Lisi," he says. "It was great."

Lisi is made woozy by a genuine thrill that explodes behind her eyes, threatening tears. "Really?"

"Yes! I'd love to talk about it—"

"Now?" Lisi presses.

"Don't you have . . ." Gabe begins, gesturing to the throng of people behind her.

"They'll be here all night getting smashed. I can come back."

Gabe smiles like he knows a very good secret and gestures toward the door. "Walk with me to the subway?"

Lisi scrambles for her duffel bag and trots behind Gabe out to the street. Mentally she begins to calculate how long she'll have with him—how many blocks to the nearest subway line that will take him uptown and how much affirmation she can wring from him in that time.

"So, what are you thinking?" Gabe says at length. "Is it poetry? Devised theater?"

"We asked ourselves that question in rehearsal but then we thought, *Is it okay if we don't really know?*" Lisi chatters. "I feel like it has moments of prose, but ideally it's more conversational?"

"The chanting felt almost ritualistic."

"Paganistic, yeah! Witchy."

"The original girl power," Gabe quips.

"Well, no," Lisi hedges, "but also like, *yes.*"

"I got that," says Gabe. "I very much felt that."

Lisi grins. "Awesome," she says on an exaggerated exhale, before realizing the happiness had knocked the wind out of her and she'd stopped walking. She has to jog to catch up and match Gabe's brisk stride. Lisi can tell Gabe is sincere in his praise because his kinetic energy was a byproduct of the engine of his very active brain. Whenever Gabe was creating, he was up and alive and unstoppable. It could not be replicated out of politeness.

"Are you familiar with Thea Benson?" Gabe asks.

"No," Lisi hesitates to admit. But Gabe seems completely undeterred by her ignorance.

"She's amazing. She paints these huge canvases right in front of you while performing these incredible spoken word pieces. Her use of repetition is mind-blowing. It's like—"

"Hypnotic?" Lisi ventures.

"Yes, but also, every time you hear the word it sounds different, somehow. It's like that Meisner exercise. Do you know what I'm talking about?"

"No."

"Google that," Gabe instructs firmly, with an illustrative jab of his thumb. "I bet your troupe would love it."

"Oh, they're not like, *my troupe* . . ." Lisi answers, suddenly embarrassed. If Gabe loved it, it would be unfair to stake sole claim to its genius. And if he hated it, which Lisi still secretly fears he might, she refuses to take responsibility for looking pedestrian in Gabe's eyes. "I mean, who knows if they're even interested in working together again."

"Well, I should introduce you to Thea, then. I think you'd really hit it off."

"Oh my god, I would die," Lisi says. "I really think I'd die."

"You should know people, Lisi. You're here. You're good. You'll keep making more."

"Of course I will," she says, with the resolute severity of an oath. She had promised Gabe the same years ago, tearfully, on the eve of his departure for New York.

"This is me," Gabe says as they turn onto Lafayette. "Thanks for walking me."

"Thank you for *coming*," Lisi exhales.

Gabe stills, an expression partway between amusement and bewilderment stretching his mouth into a thin smile. "Did you *really* think I wouldn't come?" he asks plainly, his arms crossed tight against his chest. He stands in a prim fourth position, a bit like a fencer, coiled and prepared to lunge.

Lisi grinds her heel into the cement, abashed. "I just know that you're like. A big deal."

"Lisi," Gabe says, now very serious, his body as elastic as his moods. He steps toward her with purpose. He has gone from playful bristling to looming over her, eyes gray and intense, with the overall impression of an ageless stone statue atop a fountain.

"I am not a big deal," he intones. "I'm nobody."

"To me you are," she says.

He claps his hand onto her shoulder, his grave expression melting into one of delight and mischief. "You gotta get over that," he teases, every word buoyant over the ripple of his laughter. He jostles her gently until she cracks a sheepish smile. "*You're* a big deal, chickadee."

He turns and saunters toward the bright mouth of the subway entrance. "Welcome to the party," he calls jovially over his shoulder, disappearing down the steps.

Lisi floats back to the theater in a euphoric daze. Every storefront seems illuminated, the façade of every old brick building impossibly warm and charming.

"Lisi," one of her castmates yelps as she enters. "You disappeared! The tech is saying we burnt through one of the gels. They're saying we need to pay to have it replaced."

"Jess," Lisi interrupts, waving her off with a breezy, balletic turn of her wrist, "calm down. I'll figure it out."

She glides away to the tech booth, pulling cash out of her wallet, feeling impenetrable. Feeling wholly and inarguably materialized.

Gabe and Josie meet Lisi in Brooklyn, commencing their westward escape with twenty-one days until Impact. She spots their distinctive silhouettes from a distance—Gabe's long stride and square shoulders, Josie's brisk shuffle and vigilant, roving gaze. She poses herself for their approach, angling her hip against the shiny trunk of the car and slinging her leather jacket over her shoulder.

"It's fucking hot," she trumpets. And then, noting their flushed faces and sweat-through shirts, abandons the act of bravado. "I should have picked you up."

Gabe shrugs off a small duffle bag, which Josie wordlessly lifts off the dirty sidewalk and up onto his own shoulder.

"It was faster walking," Gabe huffs, catching his breath. "Manhattan is gridlocked. Woulda been a waste of gas." He rakes a handful of black hair away from his damp forehead and pauses, revealing raised eyebrows bracketing a genuinely awed expression. "You weren't kidding about the car," he says.

The car is spacious and impeccably clean, both the sparkling coat of navy paint and shiny black wheels leaving the impression that the car was driven right off the lot.

Lisi grins. "It's nice, right?"

"It's new," Josie says, ambling around the back to inspect it.

"Like I said. Certain to get us to California."

"Brand new," Josie repeats numbly, laying his palm on the trunk. "I hope it doesn't attract attention."

"From who?" Lisi asks but is only answered by Josie's severe expression, his eyes dark and glassy. She steps back, unwilling to challenge him. He had a way of becoming especially taciturn when fixated on a certain task. Helping Gabe shakily up the stairs. Measuring out dosages of medication. Cleaning incessantly during Lisi's visits, staying busy and quiet in the kitchen.

"Got everything?" Gabe asks, closing their bags in the trunk. "We're not coming back."

Lisi shrugs back at him. "Not bringing much. What's there to take?"

"Exactly," Gabe answers, almost blithely. It piques Lisi's attention, tripping the alarm wires of *not quite right*, but she can't verbalize what about it seems so unnatural.

"And you're ready too? Josie got your meds?"

Josie looks away, red-faced. "I couldn't get in," he mutters. "Bulletproof glass."

Gabe takes Josie's hand in his own and shakes it. "Hey, Jo," Gabe invites sweetly. He repeats his name more firmly until Josie looks up at him, then takes Josie's chin between his thumb and forefinger and guides him into a fervent, insistent kiss.

Lisi's breath hitches in her throat. She looks away.

She'd known Gabe and Josie as a couple for as long as she had lived in New York alongside them. She recalled Gabe physically affectionate with Josie, arm slung around his shoulders as they walked down the street, or resting his cheek atop Josie's head as he held him in the back of a taxicab. Her visits had become less frequent as Gabe's sickness worsened. At their stilted dinners out or her aimless visits to their apartment while Gabe recuperated, Josie was more warden than lover. She'd assumed their intimacy had fizzled out—or at the very least was relegated to the rare *better times*, which she wasn't around to witness. She now began to fear it did not disappear so much as there had come a point when she had been purposefully shut out of it.

Josie clears his throat, which Lisi interprets to mean that she can stop pointedly staring at her shoes.

"I'm ready," he says, pink now from something other than the uncommon September heat.

Josie takes the driver's seat. Lisi prickles with annoyance at Josie's presumption, until she recalls Gabe's occasional migraines and her own admitted distaste for driving.

They make good time through her neighborhood, but as they approach the Manhattan Bridge, the world grows claustrophobic around them. People walk aimlessly through the traffic, winding around the stalled cars, abandoning the pedestrian walkways to cross the bridge any way they can. The closed windows do little to keep out the din of the raucous background.

They're startled by a knock against the window, just beside Lisi's head. A woman's face looms there, pink and bloated from distress. She mouths something which cannot be heard.

"What does she want?" Lisi says. Josie seems to be explicitly unwilling to give the strange woman any attention, eyes glued to the stoplight that appears committed to staying red. Gabe turns anxiously over his shoulder every time her thumping starts anew, moving from a polite knock to banging the open palm of her hand in a rapid *thak-thak-thak* against the window. Lisi cannot make any sense of her persistent babbling through the glass.

"She's really upset," Lisi says. "I'm going to roll down the window."

"Lisi, don't," Josie warns.

"What's she going to do, jump through?" Lisi snaps. She cracks the window, and they are assaulted by a wall of sound.

". . . even if I walk," the woman babbles, "it's all on highway and I don't think—"

"Hey, hey," Lisi levels with her firmly. "We couldn't hear you. Start over."

The woman clutches her backpack against her chest like it is a newborn, her thin red hair stuck untidily to her scalp and forehead from the heat. There is a wildness in her eyes, a palpable, unwieldy desperation.

She takes a shaky breath. "I'm trying to get to New Jersey. Are you going to New Jersey?"

"Are we?" Lisi asks, rapping her index finger twice on Josie's shoulder.

"It doesn't matter," Josie grunts through clenched teeth. "Roll up the window."

"Please," says the woman. "They're in Livingston. It's just past the tunnel. It's so close."

"Is that close, Josie?"

"I don't know," he says. "Lisi, the light—"

"The light is about to change," Lisi says apologetically. "Try another car?"

"I *have* tried other cars!" she clamors, clutching the rim of the open window. "I have."

Lisi looks at her expectantly.

"Other cars stopped. But you're the only . . ." She clears her throat. "You're the first car with a woman."

Lisi looks to Gabe for guidance but finds his expression infuriatingly unreadable. She yanks the car door open. The woman dives in, nearly faster than Lisi can slide over to make room for her.

"Thank you, really, thank you." The volume of her voice rises as she gibbers with relief. "I just want to get to New Jersey."

Lisi watches the woman try valiantly to catch her breath, her eyes scanning the car and their surroundings and the crawling proximity to the entrance of the bridge. She's older than all of them—maybe forty—heavyset and fair in a way that quite resembles Josie, though

Lisi doubts either of them have much interest in getting to know each other. She has cried or sweat her mascara into dark rings beneath her eyes, which pangs Lisi with a sour sort of pity.

"I'm Lisi Fish," she says. Lisi extends her hand enthusiastically. The woman's eyes lock onto Lisi's outstretched palm, but she keeps her arms folded tightly around the backpack on her lap.

"Maureen Stussy," the woman responds.

"I had a college professor here named Stussy," Lisi chirps. "I loved her. Are you related?"

"No, I told you my family is in New Jersey," she repeats, agitation spiking. "Just past the Holland Tunnel."

"I'm Gabe," Gabe interrupts, perhaps to quell the rising hysteria. "I'm Lisi's cousin. This is my boyfriend, Josie."

Josie only nods at her in the rearview mirror.

"I can tell you how to get to Livingston," she appeals to the little of Josie she can see.

"Remind me when we're through the tunnel," says Josie. "I can get us that far."

They ride in strained silence, antsy from the noise and the traffic, susceptible to the oppressive, unhappy energy of so many fleeing people. It takes nearly two tense, claustrophobic hours to inch haltingly through the dim orange lights of the Holland Tunnel. There is a collective, audible exhalation of relief as the mouth of the exit appears, with its promise of natural light and fresh air.

"Stay left here," Maureen pipes up. "We need to get on the interstate."

The highway winds off into busy arterials, arterials feeding into local thoroughfares, finally splintering off into suburban, tree-lined streets.

"I can get out here," says Maureen. "I can walk."

"It's fine," says Josie from the front. "We'll take you to your house."

"It's my parents' house," she corrects him.

Lisi places her hand on the seat between them. "We're driving to my parents' too," she ventures. "In Sacramento."

Maureen gasps. "God bless you," she says. "That's far."

Maureen directs them to the end of a row of houses along a very green, very quiet street. Two elderly people cautiously teeter down the front steps as the car approaches. Maureen leaps out of the car without a word, into the arms of the old woman. Behind them, three kindred redheads barrel out of the front door. Maureen is enveloped into their joint embrace. "I didn't know, I didn't know," someone is saying over

and over. At a certain point, Josie backs the car up and pulls away, unnoticed by the family, utterly inconsequential.

TWENTY DAYS

Traffic clears out in Pennsylvania. Freeways remain busy, but the agitated stream of exiles begins to siphon off in various directions, leaving some of the state highways less populated. By nightfall, they're able to log sufficient miles to feel good about the day's effort. Lisi is the one who remarks that it's approaching midnight, so they agree to catch a few hours of sleep parked on the roadside. All three of them rest fitfully under the bright overhead highway lights, the car rocking every time a speeding car clips past.

"I want to find a gas station today," Josie says once dawn has broken and it is clear that all three of them have abandoned the polite charade of being asleep. "Load up on supplies while we can."

"I saw a sign for stuff at the next exit," says Lisi. "Hotels and restaurants and gas stations, that kinda thing."

Josie chews his bottom lip, scanning their surroundings. The stretch of highway had remained calm, but it was still early. Sunlight would draw the crowds. "We shouldn't try anything near populated places," he rebuffs gruffly.

Lisi responds with a click of her tongue and a petulant shrug, then busies herself with her phone. They had all lost cell service somewhere around Allentown. Lisi ventured that it had something to do with the mass of humanity around them, all similarly trying to contact friends and family. But now, alone on an empty stretch of road, the signal comes up similarly blank.

"But thank you for looking out, Lisi," says Josie, by way of an apology. She does not respond.

Josie eases the car back onto the highway. Gabe drums idly on the console between them with long, pretty fingers. Josie aches to squeeze them in his palm. He considers it; Lisi seems distracted enough by her cell phone, lazing across the back seat. Her long legs are perched on the adjacent passenger seat, chunky black boots resting on the upholstery. Josie thinks to scold her but realizes it's her car, which will end up in oblivion with the rest of humanity, so what does it matter if she scuffs the leather?

She is very cool. There's a corny insufficiency to that word that embarrasses Josie a bit, even in his own head, but he's not sure what other word fits. She is cool in ways that seem both effortless and intensely studied. Gabe was cool, but possessed some other self-assured quality Josie never fully had the language to express, something both aspirational and unattainable. Where Gabe's even-keeled poise left an impression of agelessness, to Josie, Lisi seemed eternally young. Gabe had expressed, more than once, that Josie treated Lisi like a teenager. Josie always evaded the subject with some polite, hollow protestation. Gabe was correct, of course, but what could Josie say? Lisi was Gabe's proudest creation; he was protective of her in totality, even the qualities Josie chafed against.

They proceed in silence as they drive, Josie preoccupied with navigating through the local back-road thoroughfares that run parallel to the freeway. The scenery is notably different—the roadsides dense with verdant trees, and pavement rough from a lack of upkeep.

A particularly jarring pothole seems to knock Lisi's attention away from her phone. "What happened to the road?" she queries, squinting out the window. The mid-morning sun is bright now, low and full in the sky.

"We're off the highway," Josie answers. "We should start looking for convenience stores now. Something small. Small is best."

Josie watches Lisi in the rearview; her attention is already elsewhere. She tucks her feet beneath her thighs and presses her nose to the window, clouding it with a white bloom when she exhales. Light ribbons against her face as she stares out at the trees, still and heavy with late summer leaves.

"It all feels haunted already," she muses. "Doesn't it?"

"What's that?" Gabe asks, moving out of his own quiet reverie.

"Earth," says Lisi. "Do you think it knows its days are numbered?"

"I think she's blissfully unaware," Gabe answers, angling his head into the hot slat of sunlight pouring in through the easterly window. "I wouldn't wish it on her. It's exhausting to know you're dying." He chuckles at that.

Lisi traces a long finger down the length of the window. "Maybe Earth will crack apart into a thousand pieces and float through space for the rest of eternity," she says. "Or maybe it'll be like the dinosaurs all over again. Just a husk of a planet inhabited only by ghosts."

The easy poeticism does not impress Josie in the slightest. He isn't aware that he had scoffed aloud until he catches Lisi's accusatory glare in the rearview mirror.

"Well, I think it's nice," she justifies. "Life after death and all that."

"Ghosts are not life after death."

"Of course you don't believe in ghosts," says Lisi. "Religious people never do."

"I'm not religious," Josie answers, gripping the wheel.

"Oh," says Lisi. She sits quietly for a moment, watching the landscape pass. "But you *were*."

"Yes. I was raised Mennonite."

"Right!" Lisi gasps. "I listened to this NPR thing about how there's only a few left in America. It was so sad."

"That's Shakers."

"Oh, that's it," says Lisi. "Uh-huh."

Josie tries not to entertain notions of coincidence or clairvoyance, but he can't disentangle Lisi's sudden interest in his upbringing from the fact that as they approach the border of Ohio, they are passing closer to Josie's childhood home than he has ever been since he left. Even the trees begin to feel suffocatingly familiar, the particular hum of the bugs in the leaves. His foot presses heavier on the gas.

He has no reason to feel guilt about remaining estranged from an already purposefully estranged family, but it still makes him sick knowing they're all dying soon too. He cannot picture their homes or who they'll be with when the moment arrives. He doesn't know if his siblings have children. The most palpable memory of his eldest sister is of her wedding, as she tugged unhappily at the taut buttons on Josie's white dress shirt. "Josiah still hasn't lost his baby fat," she said to no one in particular, getting him in line for the wedding photos.

The sound of Lisi's voice knocks him from the memory. "Did you drive, like, a horse and buggy?"

"No," he answers quickly. "We had cars. It was exactly like your childhood," he adds, hoping to put it to rest. "I was a good kid."

Lisi sputters a laugh through her pursed lips. "*We* were not good kids."

"Really?" Josie asks. Gabe thumbs at his eyebrow and nonchalantly waves Josie's attention off, not quite obscuring the redness of his cheeks.

"You don't know?" Lisi gasps. "Gabe was the *worst*." She leans forward and drapes herself over the back of Gabe's chair, buoyant with mischief. "He had no interest in anything unless you said it was forbidden. Then Gabe became an expert on it overnight and said you were keeping him from his passion."

Gabe pushes one of Lisi's expressive hands out of his line of sight.

"I'm sure that's an exaggeration," Josie counters politely, unable to hide his growing smile. It sounds very much like something a young

Gabe would do. Gabe spoke so little of his upbringing that Josie held dear to any glimpse of who Gabe once was. And, too, was thankful to have moved past questions about his own life.

"There was actually a period where Gabe got, like, very into punk," Lisi says. "Do you remember that?"

"Hmm," Gabe hedges, pressing the knuckles of his right hand into his lips.

"Is that true?"

"Black eyeliner and hair gel and really serious poetry."

Gabe shrugs. "I was sixteen," he says, countering Josie's bemused look.

"Actually, the poetry was pretty good," Lisi continues. "I got in trouble with my parents because I told them they were 'gorging on dirt under the shoe of corporatism.'"

"Under the *heel*," Gabe corrects her, mumbling into the palm of his hand. He is turned away, staring resolutely out of the passenger-side window.

"Right, right, the heel. See? Still pretty evocative stuff."

Josie suppresses a laugh. "Evocative," he echoes, feeling the heat of Gabe's humiliation radiating off the back of his flushed neck.

"Speaking of my parents . . ." Lisi trails off, falling back into her own seat with a *thunk*. She fumbles in her bag for her cell phone again, angling it toward the windows, holding it aloft to see if it picks up service.

Taking advantage of her distraction, Josie rests his hand on Gabe's thigh, thumb settling in the divot of his knee cap. "You never told me any of these things," Josie says, trying not to sound too teasing. Embarrassment is a strange look on Gabe, and terribly endearing.

Gabe scoffs into his palm. "Wonder why." As a small concession, Gabe rests his hand atop Josie's. Josie is entranced by the neat anthills of Gabe's knuckles, slightly pink, slightly dry. He pries his attention back to the empty road ahead.

"What about your teenage years?" Gabe prods. "You never tell me anything, either."

"There's nothing to tell. I was nobody."

"Fuck," groans Lisi from behind them. "Still no cell service."

Josie keeps his eyes on the road, undeterred. There is nothing more to be said about that.

Gabe loses track of the time as they wind through quiet, rural Ohio back roads until Josie pulls into a gas station that looks abandoned. The gas pumps appear operational, the attached convenience store well-stocked. There is only the small matter of the locked doors.

Gabe first suggests throwing something through the door, but Josie argues it wouldn't be worth an alarm going off. Lisi spots a side window above the cash register left propped open, likely forgotten in the mania following the breaking news. With a bit of boasting, and a small boost from an empty crate, Lisi hauls herself up and through the open window. She jogs around to the plexiglass doors where Josie and Gabe wait for her and flings them open with evident satisfaction.

"After you, sirs," she invites in a dulcet baritone, with a flourish of her wrist. "There's so much stuff. Everything on your list, Josie."

Josie strides in past her and out of the sun.

"Should I see if the pump works?" Gabe asks.

Josie nods back at him before disappearing down an aisle full of pretzel bags and waxy packets of jerky.

"Oh, it was no trouble at all," Lisi huffs, addressing the empty spot where Josie once stood. "You're so very welcome."

Gabe claps her on the shoulder reassuringly, more amused than he cares to let on. She trots off into the darkened convenience store after Josie with one final, put-upon sigh.

The gas pumps are still functioning, so Gabe fills the tank and pays with his credit card. Every routine action feels both nonsensical and too good to be true. There's an absurd hilarity in the notion that any resources should still be meted out and paid for, and in the naked farce of accruing debt to be settled at some later date. All the same, Gabe knows there will come a time soon when resources won't come quite so easily, so he kisses his knuckles superstitiously and shakes the last few drops of gas into the tank.

Josie emerges with three large crates of bottled water. Gabe tries to assist, but Josie stubbornly wrangles them into the trunk on his own.

"You're bright red," Gabe says. Josie is, indeed, flushed from his ears down past his neck and has sweat through the front of his shirt.

"I'm fine," Josie huffs with a dismissive wave of his hand. "You should pick some food you like."

"Jo," Gabe entreats, catching Josie's wrist as he brushes past. Josie stumbles to a halt. He turns over his shoulder, startled and accusatory.

It is an expression that sits strangely in Josie's round features.

"What?" Josie says, brusquely shaking his arm out of Gabe's grasp. "You don't think I can lift a case of water?"

Josie exhales sharply. "I just want to get back on the road," Josie says. "I don't want to be seen. I don't want to . . ." He struggles for the next word, looking woefully at the road that stretches ahead of them. "I don't want to compete," he concludes. He fumbles for something rumpled emerging from his back pocket and holds a slightly wilted paper map aloft. "Can you grab some of these? As many different ones as you can find. That would be helpful."

Gabe nods and follows Josie into the darkened convenience store. He loads up his arms with outdated paper maps and bags of chips, cereal, peanuts—anything that looks even vaguely appetizing. Josie is behind the counter, pulling bottles of Advil off the shelves.

Gabe tries not to chafe at Josie's overwrought fussing. Ultimately, Josie is correct, and Gabe accepts that almost as quickly as the annoyance had frothed up inside him. They'd been lucky not to run into any other travelers thus far. Gabe shouldn't be overexerting himself for no other reason than pridefulness. At home, Gabe was invalid and Josie nurse, Gabe unemployed and Josie gainful. It'd been that way, on and off, for nearly half of their relationship. The change of pace and scenery is seductive; Gabe can't help but sprint into the boundaries.

Lisi meets them outside with a similarly unruly armful of food and two packs of cigarettes, one forcefully lodged into each of the impractically small breast pockets of her leather jacket.

"You smoke?" asks Gabe.

"Socially," she says.

"Not very good for you," Josie notes, not quite inaudibly. Gabe gets the sense that Josie's breathlessness from loading the car contributed more to the volume of his voice than a genuine desire to be heard. Josie immediately flushes, and not from exertion.

"What's it gonna do?" she chides. "Kill me?"

Josie doesn't deign to respond, sliding back into the driver's seat and slamming the door closed behind him. Once he is out of sight, Lisi summons one of her spectacular eyerolls.

"He's not wrong," Gabe contends.

"I don't even *really* smoke," Lisi says. "I haven't had a cigarette since I was like, twenty-two. I think we were at a rooftop party in Greenpoint. Do you remember that?"

"No," says Gabe.

"We shared a cigarette—it was some theater director's party," she expounds, scrabbling for the memory. "Yes! Halloween! You—"

"I don't smoke," Gabe answers tersely, and returns to the car.

He does recall the party, and the shared cigarette, and the stage-two brain cancer diagnosis that arrived not long after. At the time the news felt both profoundly karmic and utterly senseless, and had nothing at all to do with a shared cigarette on a drunken night or any other young-adult vice, but everything feels like punishment when life is punishing. Lisi stopped smoking after that too, similarly shaken by the diagnosis. Gabe was grateful she seemed to have forgotten that.

The drive picks up again in relative silence, Gabe eager to make amends with Josie in private, Lisi drifting in and out of sleep in the back seat, and Josie too locked into his missive to do anything but drive. Dusk falls around the time they cross into Indiana, rocky cliff faces rising up out of the straths on either side of the highway, the sky blanching to a fuzzy, velveteen gray. Josie stays focused on the road, brow furrowed, heavy bottom lip hung open in concentration. Gabe is overwhelmed by his desire to kiss him, to apologize for things not quite nameable and too vast to pinpoint.

Josie pulls off the highway and follows a narrow gravel road until it dead-ends in a wide, flat valley.

Gabe leans back to gently jostle Lisi's knee.

"Where're we?" she mumbles as she awakens, pushing hair out of her face.

Gabe hushes her gently as Josie removes the key from the ignition, the engine clicking and hissing as it cools.

"It's all good," Gabe says. "We're in Indiana. Have been for an hour or so."

Her eyes flit to the windows, taking in the new landscape. Josie had managed to find a flat and roadless basin, obscured by crags of rock on either side. "What's this?"

"I just pulled off the highway. I don't drive well in this kind of light," Josie says, and rolls his shoulders. "The sky starts to look like the road."

"So we'll rest," says Gabe, sliding his hand up Josie's knee. Josie seems to not even notice.

"I could take a walk," Lisi pipes up. "I'm sore."

Gabe nods his agreement, and Lisi is out of the car in an instant, loudly cracking her back and her neck. She hikes away in big, elongated strides.

"Don't go too far, it's going to get dark soon," Josie calls after her through the open window. She tosses up a dismissive hand in response but does not turn around. "Do you think she knows how fast it gets dark?" Josie frets, craning out of the window as she shuffles off, windmilling her long arms.

Gabe places his hand on the back of Josie's neck, beckoning for his attention. Josie continues to watch Lisi pace away.

"Jo, you need a break," Gabe says. "Why don't you sleep in the back seat tonight?"

Josie expels all his breath in a way Gabe is familiar with: an exhalation not of any real relief but a deliberate and practiced endeavor to find some semblance of calm. "I think I might need a stretch too," Josie says, wincing even as he turns to slide out the door. Gabe follows behind him.

"C'mere," Gabe says, extending his arm. "Let me help."

Josie approaches slowly on lock-kneed legs. Gabe angles Josie to face the car, and then steps behind him. He slides his hands around Josie, one settling atop his hip, the other resting on his stomach.

"Lean forward," Gabe says. "From the waist, like a hinge. You've seen me do it."

Josie looks over his shoulder with eyes like saucers, his mouth frozen in a pinched *o*, as though too many simultaneous thoughts had overloaded his capacity to say anything at all. Gabe feels a small, startled breath hitch under his palm. He tamps down the flutter of desire in his stomach.

"Try and rest your elbows on the car, but keep your palms together," Gabe instructs.

"Uh-oh," Josie titters but follows direction. Gabe helps adjust him, easing Josie's hips back slowly, deepening the stretch in his mid-back. Suddenly, there's a series of satisfying cracks and Josie's noise of alarm, followed by a low, rumbling groan of appreciation.

"Good?" Gabe asks.

"Mm," says Josie indelicately.

Gabe carefully takes Josie's arm and stretches it out from the rotator cuff, then the other. "Any better?"

Josie nods, hinging upright once again. He stumbles back—his knees uncooperative—into Gabe's sure and anticipatory arms. A startled apology squeaks out of him as if propelled by the impact. Gabe ducks his head, burying his nose at the crown of Josie's skull. He doesn't smell entirely pleasant—there's a musk of sweat and the stale air conditioning of the car—but there is still the familiar peppery underpinnings of what is inherently just Josie.

"You know I find you unbearably attractive," he mumbles into Josie's hair.

"Gabe . . ." Josie says in a voice that sounds entirely devoid of the chastisement he'd meant to conjure.

"I'm sorry," says Gabe.

Josie angles over his shoulder to search Gabe's expression. "For what?"

Gabe meant to apologize for the friction at the gas station earlier, for his petulance, for how much he is enjoying the freedom and change of pace while Josie could only fret over shepherding them between each temporary safety. Instead, he squeezes Josie hard. "I just love you," he says. "Please sleep."

Gabe assists Josie into the back seat, which he occupies awkwardly, unsure how to make himself comfortable.

"I'm gonna walk too," Gabe says. "Be back soon."

"Don't go too far," Josie slurs, the tiredness overtaking him. "There's no light around here."

Gabe laughs, stilling Josie's chin and pressing in for a kiss. "I got it, babe, I got it. You just lie down."

Gabe closes the car door behind him. He checks over his shoulder a handful of times as he ambles away, as if feeling the heat of Josie's worry on the back of his neck. At some point, the automatic overhead lights click off, and the darkened car nearly disappears into the dusk. Gabe ducks behind a swath of overgrown shrubbery to relieve himself. The sky is wide and unobstructed. Gabe can dizzy himself just craning up, observing nothing but the dusty gray-blue color, like a painted scrim on an old Hollywood sound stage. It makes his knees weak, dissolving into all that light.

Curious, he traipses farther down the dry, rocky gully to a stretch of flat rock. There is so much beautiful and lonely space. Gabe is enamored by it. Inspired. He pivots on his toe slowly. The gravel crunches beneath his shoe. His knee rises, hinged with his sole parallel to the ground. He feels weight in his opposite heel, firm and grounded. He extends his leg, points his toe, and rotates from the hip into a wide, open arabesque. His muscles are tight, and his knee won't lock straight like it should, the line broken by the stunted extension. But it is intoxicating to move, to know his body is still capable of it, to strain toward the neglected edges of his kinesphere. He swings his head freely, lets the momentum carry his body around and his leg back down to the earth, arms windmilling wide and then tucking against his chest. Nothing but the sound of sand and gravel and his exhalation.

He thinks of Josie worrying after him, squinting unhappily into the dusk, so he comes to a rest. His blood is pounding. He feels viciously alive.

Gabe strides back to the car quickly, feeling like he's pocketed a glittering little secret. As he slides back into the passenger seat, he notices Lisi still missing. He inhales, turning over his shoulder to ask Josie if she had been back at all yet.

Josie is laid out in the back seat, supine, his arms crossed over his chest like a well-arranged corpse. He has removed his boots, yet, inexplicably, they remain clutched protectively against his chest, the soles dirtying his shirt. Gabe cannot discern if it was an error made out of exhaustion or some considered precaution. Josie in crisis was a familiar stalwart; Josie at rest would always be a bit of a mystery to Gabe.

"Jo," he whispers, brushing the back of his fingers over Josie's cheek. His jaw stays slack, puffing out small, even breaths. Dead to the world. Gabe suddenly feels lonely and ravenous for his attention.

Lisi returns from her walk only slightly worse for wear, the pale sun fully swallowed by the distant tree line. Dusk had trickled in slowly, then pitched into opaque blackness in an instant, just as Josie had warned. Lisi found herself at the bottom of a small but very steep cleft of rock as darkness fell, and she scrabbled clumsily up the side of it for longer than she cared to admit. For a brief and childish moment, she regarded the whole undignified folly as a direct result of Josie's henpecking. She wouldn't have wandered out so far if Josie hadn't expressly demanded the opposite; small acts of rebellion were the only available response to Josie's authority. It's harder to admit that the struggle and the solitude feel an eerie portent of what is to come.

The parked car is dark and silent. She imagines Gabe and Josie already asleep inside with a small pang of jealousy. Instead of puncturing that bubble—envisioning herself apologizing for intruding, always the interloper—she climbs onto the roof of the car. Lisi folds her legs underneath her, careful not to scuff the paint with the thick soles of her boots.

The stars are dim pinpricks against a hazy indigo sky. She indulges in one of her pilfered cigarettes, away from any potential judgment, and pulls out her cell phone once more.

"Psst," comes a voice. "Do you have service?"

Lisi startles and the cell phone nearly tumbles out of her hand.

Craning out of the open passenger-side window is Gabe, his toothy grin white in the low light.

"Gabe, oh my god," she chastises. "You scared me."

"You're smoking?" he asks, jutting his chin toward the palm splayed against her thudding heart, lit cigarette pinched between the knuckles of her index and middle finger.

"Are you mad? I can go somewhere else."

"Not at all. Can I come up?"

She nods enthusiastically, and Gabe's face disappears back into the car. Gingerly, he opens and shuts the door behind him and then, with an almost practiced facility, plants both feet onto the front tire and hoists himself gracefully onto the roof.

"Not bad, right?" Gabe says, apparently deeply self-satisfied by his performance. Lisi raises her cigarette as if toasting a glass.

He settles next to her. It's slightly too narrow for comfort atop the car, but there's a crispness in the air, and the cold rock surrounding them seems to hold the chill. It's nice to sit hip-to-hip, his warm forearm pressed against her own.

"Josie's out like a light," Gabe says.

"He drove all day," Lisi answers, and in saying it aloud realizes the rigor of that task. She briefly tussles with guilt, wondering if she should have volunteered to take over. But she also knows Josie would never have let her. Gabe seems to have followed her train of thought and rolls his eyes affectionately. Lisi chortles, lifting her hand for another long drag from her cigarette. She carefully ashes it away from Gabe.

"Can I have one?" he asks.

"Really? Didn't you say—"

"I was lying, I have smoked. A few times in college. Sometimes I'd travel to perform and felt lonely in the bars after shows." Gabe shrugs. "It was an easy way to join a crowd. Don't tell Josie?"

Lisi raises a skeptical eyebrow. "About now or then?"

"Both," he answers firmly. "Deal?"

She wrestles the pack out of her cropped leather jacket, shakes another cigarette out, and proffers it toward Gabe. He accepts it with equal flourish and lights it with an ease that belies his minimal experience. Lisi is aware of his theatrical talent for making things look easy, but this makes her laugh.

"Yes, very cool," she commends, knowing Gabe would eventually needle her for an acknowledgment. He smiles around his cigarette.

He exhales deeply, gratefully, rolling his neck and shoulders as the smoke curls up and away, revealing his face again. He is still smiling, alight with a crackle of mischievous energy.

"Finally," Gabe says. "A bad idea you're imposing on *me*."

"What are you talking about?"

"That's historically been my job. Like how you moved to New York for me."

"Not *for* you," says Lisi. "I moved to New York for my career."

"And remember when I convinced you we should get tattoos on St. Mark's Place, next to that yakitori shop?"

"I like my tattoo," Lisi counters sincerely.

"It cost twelve dollars, and we had to wait outside in the alley. That's exclusively for drunk college kids and idiots."

Lisi shrugs at that. "We *were* drunk. And I *was* in college."

Lisi recalls being splayed out in the tattoo parlor chair with her tight jeans rolled up around her shin, giggling, "This is so stupid, this is so stupid," and never breaking eye contact with Gabe as the artist hunched over her bare ankle. Looking to him, as she always had, for approval, for the next dare, for the gratifying warmth of his company.

"And also," Lisi continues. "We *are* idiots."

"I told you that you should apply to college for the arts. That's a bad idea."

"Okay, well, I actually built my own major," she protests. "So. There's a lot of use there."

Gabe tucks his knees up to his chest and drapes over them dramatically. "You have an answer for everything."

"I'm not being stubborn, if that's what you're implying. None of these were bad ideas." She takes a moment to consider what they are and concludes, "They're cool."

Gabe grins at her sideways, his temple resting on his tented knees. "You think I'm cool?" he singsongs teasingly. But there's an expectation in his expression, in his unblinking dark eyes, that tells Lisi that he sincerely wants an answer.

"You know I think you're cool," Lisi says, embarrassment swelling her tongue and softening her cadence. Her voice emerges warm and marble-mouthed. "Everything you do, I envy."

Gabe puffs up. He places his palm on the dome of her head and musses her hair.

She jerks out of the reach of his arm. "Gabe!" she yelps.

"Shh, shh," Gabe overlaps her, giddy, his finger to his lips. "Josie's asleep."

"I'd be so much angrier if we still had mirrors," she says in a theatrical whisper, fingering through her bangs to right them. Even at the end of civilization itself, Lisi would still be crestfallen to be caught looking any kind of sloppy that wasn't deeply intentional. It earns a fond chuckle from Gabe, but no assistance.

Finally mollified, Lisi turns her attention back to Gabe, sitting contented with his chin fitted neatly in his palm. "Can I say something?"

"Hit me," he says.

Lisi looks at him squarely, hugging her knees to her chest. "You seem . . . I dunno. Happy."

"I am happy," Gabe answers without pause. "I'm out of my apartment. I'm with you and Josie, and I love you both. I don't know what to say."

"You're not scared?"

"I've been about to die for a while," answers Gabe, without much sentiment. "This doesn't feel all that different."

Lisi flicks the butt of her cigarette off the side of the car with a tight, drawn breath. "Was it really that soon?" she asks.

Gabe shrugs. "The latest news wasn't particularly good."

"Just 'not particularly good'?" Lisi asks, feeling a cold dread beginning to prick at the base of her neck. "Or actively bad?"

Gabe rolls his eyes, seemingly hiding a laugh behind the cigarette raised to his lips. "Bad. Actively." He inhales deeply and exhales a substantial cloud of spiraling white smoke. Gabe's eyes are cast heavenward, watching it dissipate. "Maybe six months?"

Lisi gasps before she can think any better of it. Her instinct to reject bad news bicycles madly inside her, making her feel both lightheaded and bitterly guilty.

"Could have been more," Gabe continues brightly, seemingly unoffended by her speechlessness. "Maybe less. I don't know. But the tumors are growing at a certain rate, and at some point they're going to start impacting the parts of my brain necessary to function."

Lisi tries to logic her way out of her queasiness. She doesn't need to know what that means, what functions would be stripped from him, and when, and what kind of Gabe that would leave behind for her to love. They wouldn't have to cross that road.

"Once I told my doctor I wasn't interested in pursuing further treatment, we started talking about hospice care, so Josie wouldn't have to play full-time nurse." Gabe rolls the extinguished butt of his cigarette between his fingers. "Killed that fast," he muses, tossing the remnants into the darkness rapidly pooling around their car. "I meant the mood, not the cigarette."

"I didn't know," Lisi says numbly. "You seem so . . ."

"Healthy?" Gabe suggests.

"Yeah," she answers. Lisi bites down on her thumb nervously. "Sorry. Is that bad of me to say?"

Gabe touches her knee affectionately, a languid shrug lifting his broad, coat-hanger shoulders. "I want you to think I'm healthy," he says. "I wanted to feel healthy, for at least a little while."

"So what did Josie say?" Lisi asks. "He didn't seem to be acting any differently. I thought he'd be—"

Gabe suddenly stiffens, sucking in a breath through his teeth. "He doesn't know," says Gabe. "And you can't tell him, Lisi."

"Gabe," she rebuts, warningly. "No fucking way. I have never successfully kept a secret, and this is the *mother lode* of all fucking secrets."

"It's not a secret," Gabe says. He turns his gaze on her, steely and impenetrable. "It's a kindness. It used to matter a lot, and now it doesn't matter anymore."

"*How* doesn't he know?" Lisi splutters. "Doesn't he like . . . stalk your phone calls? Come to every doctor's appointment?"

Gabe raises his eyebrow pointedly. Lisi is wise enough to clack her jaw closed and shut up.

"Of course I was *going* to tell him," Gabe says. "But you don't tell someone bad news unless it's certain. I had an appointment on the books with my oncologist for next week." He inhales thoughtfully and rephrases, "I guess I mean this week. Well, obviously there's no more appointment."

He gestures vaguely toward the sky, turning his open hand as if conjuring something, summoning the calamity that has not quite arrived. Lisi understands his meaning.

"It's the luckiest thing that could happen to me," he says. "You know. Personally."

He laughs at Lisi's dropped jaw.

"I wouldn't have *chosen* it at the sake of the whole of humanity, if I were in the driver's seat. But I'll take what I can get."

Lisi supposes it is, ultimately, a selfish thing to say. But she can't imagine feeling any other way in his position. They sit in silence for a long moment, studying the sky.

"Thank you for taking me to see my parents," Lisi says. Her voice is low and gravely from the brisk air and the cigarette. "I know you don't love being home."

Gabe shifts, manages a half-hearted shrug, but otherwise says nothing.

"I'm not expecting you to play nice with anyone you don't want to see," Lisi continues.

"Don't worry about that," says Gabe. He smirks at her. "Besides, you couldn't have made me."

Lisi reaches out, placing her hand on Gabe's shoulder. "I still want to, um . . ." She clears her throat, which has pinched tight around her timorous voice. "To be with you. At the end. I'm sure we'll figure something out."

"'Course, Lisi. You always would've been with me at the end," Gabe assures her. "It's just coming a little sooner for all of us."

Lisi smiles. She hopes that's true—that she would have been there through all of it, the worst of it, the ugly and inexorable end.

"We have to take care of Josie," Gabe says. The sky has darkened, and it's hard to see Gabe now without the meager, warm glow from their cigarettes. His eyes are downcast, or perhaps closed. Lisi cannot tell. "I know it seems like he has it all together. He's going to run and run and run, but no matter what he does, there's no beating this one. He's going to be terrified."

I'm terrified, Lisi wants to protest, but at that moment she feels strangely at ease, and so seemingly does Gabe. So instead she says, "I will."

Gabe turns and pats her twice, bracingly, on her cheek. It makes her realize she's gotten quite cold and wants to get back into the cocoon of their car.

"Thanks, chickadee," says Gabe, and with the miraculous ability to always act first, he pivots and leaps off the roof of the car. He extends a hand back up toward Lisi. "Jump," he says, closing his hand around her wrist. "I gotcha."

Lisi knows it's silly, but she jumps.

They start the morning with radio. Josie has noticed radio activity dies down as the day progresses and nights are nothing but static no matter how much he skims. The broadcasts are varied and unsanctioned, some dedicated to breaking news, others dispatching desperate messages into the void—*Marco, we made it to Chicago*—*Lily, baby, this is Mommy. If you hear this we are leaving for Paducah*—

Josie skims until he finds a recognizable voice from the previous day's broadcasts. This time, the speaker is joined by a second man.

"We should enjoy the convenience, for however long it lasts."

"And how long do you think it will last?" the familiar voice asks.

"With nineteen remaining days, we're already seeing pockets without electricity. We can assume their power stations were intentionally shut down. For those still with power, understand that stations, generators, these only work with routine maintenance. Even if they were purposefully left on before evacuated—and we can be thankful for that—I won't assume anyone is spending these last days doing maintenance. But maintenance will be needed, and that's when we can expect to see the first interruptions in service."

"Should we be concerned about these empty plants? Do we run risks of meltdowns? Fires?"

"It's difficult to imagine a calamity of that nature will occur sooner than our, ah, imminent jeopardy."

It is very nearly a funny thing to say. So starkly absurd. The merits of weighing any danger in the face of certain obliteration.

"Beyond that," he continues, "we are unsure how any dramatic change in gravity, temperature, or atmosphere might affect—"

Josie clicks away from the broadcast there.

The day is spent heading south through Illinois, and night creeps purple over the hazy mountaintops just as they pass into Missouri. Gabe is quiet. His hand twists and fumbles on the console between them like a disoriented bug, as though seeking out Josie's hand, but both of Josie's hands are planted cautiously on the wheel.

Josie notes his movement out of the corner of his eye. Floundering but aping at casual. Josie knows Gabe well enough to suss out his underlying panic; he won't even meet Josie's eyes, instead staring into the middle distance.

"What is it?" Josie asks, trying to keep alarm out of his voice.

"I just can't really, um," Gabe begins, then pauses as if ashamed. "I can't see."

"Fully?" Josie asks.

"No, I can see about as far as my hand," he answers and demonstrates with a half-hearted flex of his fingers just before his nose.

"That's not good," Josie says. "Did you do anything different yesterday?"

He'd smoked with Lisi but roundly refuses to admit to that. "I just need some sleep, baby," Gabe assures him. "Keep driving. I'll close my eyes."

It is a familiar routine for the both of them: Gabe feigning nonchalance, adamant every symptom will resolve itself; Josie equally resolute that it will not, dipping into obsessiveness, unappeasable until all is set right.

"We should pull over," Lisi pipes up from the back. Her hand appears in Josie's periphery, waving toward the side of the road. "Lots of trees. I'm sure we could park where no one can see us."

Josie is too startled to respond—not because he'd forgotten about her presence, but because he had not expected Lisi to align with him. Gabe seems equally surprised, clearing his throat before managing a clipped, "Chickadee, it's nothing. It happens to me all the time."

"It doesn't sound like nothing," Lisi answers. "You can't *see*."

"You need a bed," Josie says.

Lisi immediately echoes with an affirming, "Right, exactly, we should find a bed."

Lisi cranes over Josie's shoulder, pointing down the dark stretch of highway. "Do you see that? That sign says there's lodging at the next exit."

"I can sleep in the back seat."

"You need rest. *Real* rest," Josie says pointedly. "A bed and medicine and a good night's sleep, and it'll all be fine."

"No one is going to be working at a hotel anymore," Gabe protests.

"So then it'll be empty," says Lisi. "Right, Josie?"

Josie makes a low grunt in the back of his throat. Gabe seems to be staring through him, as if willing Josie to come into focus. Josie is privately thankful Gabe cannot study him in his usual incisive way; he can feel that he's bitten through the skin worrying at his lower lip, and that his forehead is wet with sweat.

"We'll find out," Josie says and veers off the highway.

They wind off the exit ramp and side roads, under the pulsating wash of passing overhead lamps, until the navigation empties them out onto a stretch of quiet local highway. Off to one side, there are empty fast-food restaurants and auto shops with blackened windows. On the other side of the highway is a long strip of roadside motels, separated by abandoned convenience stores and empty gas stations.

But in the midst of the eerie stillness, certain pockets have become very deliberately inhabited, where every light has been switched on in an entire building, and the parking lots overrun with crowds. Groups of stragglers pass in and out of the abandoned lobbies of hotels and restaurants. Josie can feel the shape of their voices against the windows as they drive slowly past, like the round pulsating hum of locusts in tall grass, occasionally punctuated by a high, sharp voice—a laugh, a shout, indiscernible between anger and delight. It all has the sense of some sinister party, something only permitted because it could not be stopped.

Josie shudders. "Let's keep looking up ahead."

They follow the road another mile or so, avoiding where crowds seem to congregate. The population dwindles as the road narrows and the streetlights become sparse.

A small one-story motel, dark and presumably empty, sits off a short fork in the road. Josie circles the car around it twice. It is hard to discern if its state of deterioration is because of the sudden evacuation, or if it had long been that way. No doors seem broken down, and the windows remain intact. A large painted sign proclaiming *Econochoice: The Gateway to Big Spring*, slightly angled, juts out over two rusted telephone booths.

Gabe's annoyance at being overruled seems to fizzle away as he becomes increasingly indisposed, and he now slumps, silent, against the passenger-side window. The lodgings would have to do.

Josie parks beneath the low-hanging branches of a bent tree, hoping to obscure the car.

"I'll go see if I can get a room open," Lisi says.

"I'm coming," Josie volunteers.

"Stop it, I'll be fine," she interrupts. "Stay with Gabe." Just as promptly, she darts out of the car.

Josie watches her through the windshield, going down the line of motel doors, wrestling with each doorknob. She stops and seems to fixate on a door that bows as she pushes her shoulder against it. She steps back to inspect it.

"There's probably keys behind a—" Josie calls out of the window, at the exact moment when Lisi plants her heavy boot just below the knob and kicks the door in. It swings open, almost defeatedly, on rusty hinges. She turns back toward the car, grinning and waving both arms wildly over her head as if marshalling in an airplane.

Josie helps Gabe out of the car slowly, Gabe's arm slung around Josie's shoulders. They take careful, coordinated steps together.

"How about that?" Lisi crows proudly as they approach, gesturing them inside.

The room leaves much to be desired. The wallpaper peels away from the ceiling at the corners, and there is a stale musty smell hanging on the carpets and drapes. But there are two beds, and the water runs, and it is the most space they've had to themselves since leaving New York.

Josie helps Gabe out of his shoes and pants and onto the bed they'll share. Gabe falls back against the pillows leadenly, more incapacitated than he'd let on.

"Gabe?" Josie says, kneeling beside him. "I'm going to get medicine from the car."

"Mm," says Gabe, eyes pressed tightly shut.

"Don't fall asleep yet."

"Okay," Gabe mumbles. He lifts his palm to cover his eyes and says nothing else.

Lisi emerges from the bathroom and Josie shushes her preemptively. Wild-eyed, she shrugs back at him, innocent of any noisy transgressions. In moments of high drama, Josie can see in her the vestiges of Gabe as a petulant teenager.

"I'm going to go smoke," she mouths exaggeratedly. She points twice, sharply, toward the open door, then pats her breast pocket containing the pack of cigarettes.

Josie watches her stalk away into the darkness. He wants to call after her to keep her guard up, but figures there's only so many times he can say it before she ends up throttling him.

He pushes his fingers though Gabe's hair, damp with cool, clammy sweat. "I'm only leaving for a second," Josie whispers. "I'm getting your pills." Gabe does not react; he only exhales heavily through his nose. Both of Josie's stiff knees crack as he stands and follows after Lisi into the darkness to fetch Gabe's myriad medications from the car.

The night air is thick and cold and low, swollen clouds obscure the moon. Josie stops in his tracks.

"Lisi?" he calls out, but there is no response. The parked car remains a few paces away behind the old bowed tree. As the wind churns, so do its spindly, naked branches, which scrape against the windshield. Josie listens hard for anything else. He turns back, scanning down the line of closed doors leading up to the one cracked ajar where Gabe sleeps.

Something sits in his throat like a stone, making it hard to draw in breath. Josie is well acquainted with his survival instincts—he recognizes the familiar weight of someone's attention on him from afar. The skin on his forearms aches with how his hair stands on end. He rubs at his tired eyes, wills some danger to unveil itself. But nothing has changed. No new lights turned on inside the building. No sound of footsteps on gravel.

He feels something crack hard into his left cheek. The pain blossoms all at once, so shocking and so sudden that he can't even scream. His vision goes white, and then entirely dark, as he crumples to the ground. Weight presses hard into his lower back, crushing the air out of him. The sensations are frightening and incomprehensible—he can't make sense of the pain in his eye in tandem with the pressure on his spine and how he ended up on the cold, sharp gravel. It takes him time to realize that someone is on top of him, and that he's been struck.

"Gabe?" Josie gasps. His voice sounds like it has been shaken out of him, his teeth rattling in his skull.

His arms are wrenched into the small of his back. The weight on his back lifts, and Josie sucks in a grateful breath, but the discomfort in his shoulders only intensifies. With a spasmodic jerk, Josie realizes his hands have been bound.

The panic sets in. He is too weak to wrench himself up off his stomach, vision still swimming back into focus.

"Gabe!" he tries to shout, but it comes out strangulated and small. "Gabe!"

He kicks out his legs and they connect with something. Someone. They say nothing, but Josie feels hands fist into the back of his shirt and hair, and he's dragged on his stomach across the pavement, back toward their motel room. He is tossed through the threshold, landing hard on his ribcage with an audible grunt.

Josie can't see much but he can hear Gabe leap out of bed, shouting, "What? What? Who is that? Who's there?"

Josie strains toward Gabe's voice, but hardly has the strength to lift his head. He feels leaden, dizzy, his cheek stinging where it skidded across the carpet moments ago. He thinks, *All I need to do is scream. If I can just scream!*

There is the unmistakable sound of a pistol being cocked.

The air in the room changes. Josie can see the blurred shape of Gabe raising his hands above his head in surrender. "I'll do what you want," Gabe says in a very even monotone. "Just tell me."

"You've got money," the stranger barks, more a demand than a question. His voice is flat and croaky. "Get it."

"I," Gabe begins, his splintering voice betraying the cool temperament Gabe adopts under stress. "I can't really see."

"What? Are you blind?"

"He's sick," wheezes Josie from the floor. "Just let me go, I'll get you whatever you want!"

The man pushes the toe of his shoe into Josie's cheek to quiet him. "I've got time," the man says. "I know you can find your wallets."

Gabe lowers his arms and extends them in front of himself, maneuvering away from the safety of the bed. Josie strains to follow Gabe's movement from the floor. Gabe paws at the bedside table, then moves over to the top of the chest of drawers. He finds his wallet beside the lamp and holds it aloft compliantly.

"Good," the man says. "And the other one?"

The longer the man hovers above him, the more certain Josie is that he is high on something; he crackles with manic energy one second and then sways, dizzy and sluggish, the next.

Gabe continues to fumble haltingly around the perimeter until he finds Josie's wallet on the opposite bedside table.

"Tha's it," the man affirms, slipping back into lethargy, as if through a Novocain-numbed mouth. "Now you give 'em both to me."

Josie's stomach roils at the indignity of that request. "He can't *see*," he seethes. He struggles again to right himself, trying to maneuver weight onto his knees, but the boot against his cheek grinds down hard enough for something in his jaw to audibly crunch. Both wallets land on the floor—one right after the other—just in front of Josie's nose, no doubt surrendered quickly as a measure to stop both Josie and the intruder from doing something more fatally stupid.

Josie sucks in a deep, relieved breath as the man lifts his foot and stumbles forward to collect the items on the floor. The act of locating each wallet and stooping down to pocket them seems to wind the man, who unrolls into a fully upright position very slowly, as if his head was a great, unruly weight.

"I saw a car out there," he says once the wallets are tucked into his jacket. "Get me the keys."

Gabe and Josie are silent. The keys are in Josie's pants pocket, which is where they usually remain whenever they leave the car.

"*Well?*" the man presses and shakes his wrist at Gabe, the pistol rattling in his grip.

There's a guttural shout from the open doorway behind them. Then, chaos.

The man collapses to his knees, cursing and clawing at his face. Taking advantage of his agonized confusion, Lisi darts forward and lands a frantic kick to the back of his head, stunning him. He slumps forward over Josie, finally silent.

"Fuck!" Lisi screams. "Oh! God! Fuck that guy!"

"Help me up, help me up," Josie shouts, kicking his trapped legs out from under the fallen man.

"Oh my god, oh my god," Lisi repeats. She seems winded from the action, frozen as she surveys the messy aftermath of her moment of bravery. Her eyes dart from the unconscious intruder to Josie, red-faced and writhing in his restraints, to Gabe, blinking owlishly in her direction.

"I didn't kill him, right?" she squeaks.

"Lisi, what did you do?" Gabe urges in an exaggerated whisper, as though afraid of rousing the man. It seems Lisi knocked him soundly unconscious.

"Mace," she says. She lifts her keychain to demonstrate, the small attached can of mace swinging ominously beneath a jumble of keys held together by a studded black leather ornament.

"You have mace?"

"Gabe, I live in Bushwick," Lisi answers with the clipped curtness of having to explain the obvious. "Of course I have mace."

"Lisi!" Josie clamors, vying for her attention. "Please!"

Lisi snaps into action, hooking her hands under Josie's arms to haul him upright. As soon as his feet are underneath him, Lisi spins him into a forceful hug that nearly winds him. She cups both hands around his cheeks, pulling back to inspect him.

"He hit you!"

"I'm fine," says Josie.

"Your eye!"

"I'm really fine. Please, can you . . . can you figure out my hands?"

Lisi fumbles with her handful of keys. She scurries behind Josie and begins sawing desperately at the plastic zip tie. He can feel her breathing heavily on the back of his neck as she works, the action becoming faster and more desperate with each failed attempt. A mournful, wounded sound of upset ekes out of her throat. As she steps back around to face him, Josie is shocked to find her weeping, fat tears spilling over her cheeks. Josie has no idea what to make of the outpouring of emotion, whether it's concern, or fear, or the last vestiges of her adrenaline sloughing off.

"I can't cut it!" she blubbers.

"It's fine. It's fine. We'll find a knife. Just get Gabe to the car. Can you do that?"

"Yeah," she says, wiping her sleeves over her eyes brusquely. "I can."

She circles the room, filling her arms with whatever she can—their bags, the discarded clothes, Gabe's shoes—and then takes Gabe gingerly by the elbow.

"Our wallets," Gabe gasps, pulling back. "He still has them."

"Don't touch him," Lisi admonishes, at the same instant Josie babbles, "No, no, just get out of here!"

"I have my wallet," Lisi says. She looks to Josie, sober and conspiratorial, the frothing hysteria from moments earlier jettisoned entirely. "I have more than . . . I have enough for all of us."

Sometimes her expressions seem so perfect to Josie, so complete in their intensity, that he cannot separate Lisi the Person from Lisi the Actor, her handsome face like a diorama one could study and Josie the unwitting scene partner, made malleable by her huge emotions.

She pins his gaze until Josie nods his understanding. It feels strange to forfeit himself to her care, but Josie swallows back his concern and allows her to escort Gabe away. Gabe slings his arm around Lisi's neck for stability and turns to say something, inaudible to Josie, into Lisi's ear. In response, she pats his ribcage reassuringly, twin silhouettes in the darkness.

Josie follows them to the car parked under the low canopy of trees, waddling stiffly with his still-bound hands behind him. Lisi helps retrieve the car keys from his pocket, then slots both men into the car with extreme caution: Gabe first into the back seat, and then Josie into the passenger side. She cups her hand over Josie's bruised temple to be certain it won't bump against the door frame as he slumps into the seat. Before it occurs to Josie that he should thank her, she's settling behind the wheel for the first time.

"Sick bastard," Lisi mutters under her breath as they turn out of the parking lot and back onto the highway. She accelerates a little too fast for Josie's comfort, but he is too tired to say anything about it.

They drive in silence, save for Lisi's agitated breathing.

"I shouldn't have let us stay there," Josie says into the tense silence.

"No, Josie," Lisi insists. Her hand finds his shoulder and clasps it forcefully. "You are not responsible for that. Okay? We're just trying to survive."

"Yeah," says Josie hollowly. She is right, but self-flagellation is easier to comprehend than the notion that it is all out of his control, and something else could rob him of Gabe at any moment. Emptied of his adrenaline, Josie's hands have begun to go numb. He twists uncomfortably in his seat.

"He is too," says Gabe from behind them. Josie is startled that he is conscious at all.

"What?"

"Trying to survive. He has no idea what to do."

"What are you talking about?" Lisi says, jerking her head back over her shoulder. Gabe has his legs tucked tight against his chest, sightless gaze set out of the window, peering into the inky darkness.

"He just found out he's dying," says Gabe. "They all have."

They shift back into uncomfortable silence, Lisi ushering them through the night.

Josiah is home before sundown, but with little sense of the actual time. The September sun still seems endless and relentlessly warm. He had scrubbed his face clean next door, which he routinely did once dismissed from his daily work, though the day is so hot that he can no longer discern if the wetness at his brow is the vestiges of that or a new sheen of sweat.

He drops his backpack by the stairs and pushes the heels of his hands against his eyes until he is rushed by whorls of white light. The house is old, lived in by generations of Rempels, and it creaks and heaves with little provocation. Josiah finds it easy to stop and breathe along with it. He stays there, focusing on nothing but the space between his eyes, until something collides, hard, into his hip.

He stumbles back, steadying himself on the railing. "Lottie," he barks. "You could've hurt me."

"Jo-si-ah," she whines, each syllable a rolling peak and valley, "were you listening to me?"

"What, Lottie?"

"Anna and I are hungry," she explains curtly, pinching the skin above his wrist to keep his attention. She'd adopted Josiah's bossiness as soon as she was able to string sentences together, taking to marshalling little Anna about like a family pet. "Can you please make us food?"

"Mom left you sandwiches," Josiah says. "I saw it myself."

"But it's not what we want to eat, Jojo," she grouses, her diplomacy turning on a dime. "We were waiting for *you*."

"So then what is it you want?"

"Tomato soup and toast," Lottie chirps. "Please?"

"You know how to use the stove. I know you can."

"I don't like to use the can opener."

"You can be a big girl," Josiah directs, turning away.

Lottie darts between Josiah and the staircase, casting her arms out wide enough that she blocks any space between the wall and the railing.

"Please, Jojo," she appeals, abandoning the character of bullish lawyer and fully embracing put-upon desperation, doe-eyed and piteous. "I've been a big girl all day. I've been so good with Anna, even though she broke the remote, not me."

She wobbles on tip-toes as if to square off against him evenly, and he takes the plump moon of her face between his hands. Even though he's nearly a decade her senior, they look remarkably alike, and not quite like the rest of their lank, willowy family.

"Go find Anna," Josiah concedes. "And set the table."

She gasps and tears up the stairs on all fours, whooping for her sister's attention—a long, high siren-call of *Aaaannna*. Josiah cannot mask his amusement, wondering when Lottie will outgrow the silly habit and, simultaneously, hoping it won't come anytime soon. Lottie is only eight but conducts herself much older than her years, in part due to the responsibility she took at home over her younger sister. The rest of her manner is what she had absorbed from Josiah: the unbending pragmatism, the way he spoke to the children like little adults. Pressure had sanded away Josiah's foolishness. He can't even recall anything particularly foolish or childish from his own youth.

Lottie returns with little Anna in tow, and the two lay out the tableware around the worn kitchen table with incredible conscientiousness.

The meal preparation is simple and routine. Josiah slots a triangle of buttered bread into Lottie's soup and carries the bowl to her.

"Don't let my bread touch," Anna demands, jabbing her finger at Lottie's offending bowl. "It gets wet."

"Say please," Lottie corrects her.

Anna wails, "I *said* please!"

"Anna!" Lottie scolds. "Your *manners*!"

Anna screws up her little red face, but instead of devolving into childish hysterics, she huffs a short breath out of her nose and says, "Josiah, please. Please don't let my bread get wet."

"That's better," Josiah appraises, and Lottie pats Anna's hand in recognition of her herculean effort. The girls descend on their dinner, however, without manners. It nearly flatters Josiah. He can remember a time when he resented the notion of additions to the family, cramped in their small and outdated family home, more mouths to feed, more money he would need to earn after school, more noise at the end of a long day. He is abashed, staggered by his love for them, and how any iota he expends is reflected back at him tenfold. They don't clamor for their mother's food. They don't huddle at the door anticipating their older sisters' arrivals.

"Why are you late, Jojo?" Lottie slurs, spoon resting on her bottom lip.

Josiah busies himself at the sink, pondering vaguely if he's expected to prepare dinner for the rest of the family. His parents were frequently kept late closing up at the store, and his two eldest sisters are likely still at school and would be until much later, assisting with their various worship choirs and social clubs. Popularity found them easily, or they managed to craft it around themselves, with their artistic instincts and pretty faces. They were never expected home or set to any chore; it was much more important to be well-regarded and, soon, sought-after spouses.

"I'm not any later than I usually am," he says. "You're just hungry."

"You were next door?"

"Like always."

"What do you do when you go visit Mister Edigers?"

"Shopping. Cleaning."

Lottie huffs, looking sour. "It takes such a long time."

"Lot of chores to be done," says Josiah. "Be grateful it isn't you who has to do them."

"Why can't Sue go? Or Etta?"

"Mister Edigers is a single man," he explains, prickling with annoyance. "Wouldn't be right for them to go alone."

Lottie seems to consider that for a moment. "I think you should say to Mister Edigers that you want to come home straight away from now on."

"I can't do that," he says, taking her empty bowl to the sink.

"Why not?"

"Because he needs assistance since his accident," Josiah explains curtly. "And he pays me good money to do his chores."

"And we need good money," she parrots in exactly Josiah's way. She sighs loudly, rising from her chair.

"Josiah is so lucky," Anna proclaims, resting her chin in her plump palm. "You have money and you never have to share your clothes or your room."

"*And* Mister Edigers said he'll give Jojo his car next year," Lottie rambles eagerly, skipping around the circumference of the table. "Because Josiah is doing such a good job driving it already when he picks up his groceries."

"Josiah is *so* lucky," Anna repeats, drumming the table emphatically with her spoon.

"Suppose I am," says Josiah. He lays his palm atop Lottie's head, pinching one white-blonde curl between his fingers. "Will you take care of Anna's dishes when she's finished?"

"Yes, Jojo," she says, righting her posture self-seriously. "And then I have math homework."

"And who's problem is that, I wonder?" Josiah asks, thumbing the indignant jut of her sudden scowl.

He takes his backpack upstairs to his room and shuts the door behind him. His bedroom overlooks Mister Ediger's few acres of farmland, but Josiah largely keeps the curtains drawn. The house is quiet, save for its usual heaving and the muffled chatter of Anna and Lottie downstairs.

And then, in the quiet, the floor rises to meet him. His knees fold and his chest sinks through them, through the bone and through the floor and through the kitchen beneath, and the dirt under that, and Josiah is nowhere at all. Nowhere and watching himself too, from above his own body, hunched over himself on the bedroom floor, shoulders tremoring, face in his hands, his hiked-up shirt collar disguising a purpling bruise sucked into the back of his neck.

"Josie."

He plods uncertainly into wakefulness. There's a breeze against the right side of his face. He strains to open his left eye, but it's swollen shut.

"Hey, Josie," Lisi repeats more firmly. "Sorry to wake you."

He rolls in his seat to face her. The passenger-side door has been swung open, and Lisi is leaned over him, looking pleased with herself.

"Hm?" Josie says, which is as much intelligent thought as he can currently muster.

"Sorry it took so long," she says. "You and Gabe were asleep, so I didn't want to pull over until it was light out."

She pulls a Swiss army knife out of her pants pocket.

Josie surveys the landscape behind her. They've parked in an empty lot somewhere, their car surrounded by a sea of concrete, an abandoned strip mall beyond that.

"Where'd you get that?"

"Doors were already busted down," Lisi says, jutting her chin back at the abandoned Target behind her. "It was basically totally stripped. You were right about getting food early. Turn around."

"Please be careful," Josie whimpers, though he has little choice but to trust her. Lisi crouches behind him, sawing delicately at the zip tie flush against his wrists. He can hear her breathing heavily.

"Fuck," she huffs, "The knife isn't very sharp."

Josie tries to twist in his bindings, providing some slack. It only pinches his skin more.

"Had to break a display case for this shit," she quips, but it doesn't hide the strain in her voice.

There is a clipped squeal of triumph, and the zip tie splits under one final saw. Josie groans as his wrists fall apart, the blood rushing back into his hands all at once. The cold, prickling sensation takes his breath away, leaves him lightheaded, flooded with relief. It feels as if some tether inside him has also been snapped clean through. Tremendous, messy tears fall into his lap, pouring out of his eyes.

He stays turned away, endeavoring to hide his face from Lisi.

But the weeping is unruly and unstoppable; powerless to curtail it, he can only ride it out.

Lisi is kind enough to let him do so in silence. Once he's wrangled back control of his own functions, he turns to her and thanks her. She looks only moderately frightened.

"And here," she says, shaking a bottle of aspirin that she pulls out of her jacket. "I think you'll probably want this."

Before he can ask for one, Lisi is pushing a bottle of water into Josie's hand. He pinches four painkillers out of the container and swallows them down gratefully. He hadn't realized how much his head was throbbing.

"Thank you, Lisi," he gulps. "This was very considerate."

Lisi flinches. "I'm a good person, Josie," she says, chuckling, but her expression belies that she finds any humor in her assertion at all.

The sun is rising behind their car, the sky melting from pale blue into a shocking array of reds and pinks and oranges. Lisi and Josie watch it rise over the tree line in silence.

Gabe is contorted in the back seat, his knees against his chest, head bent back at an unusual angle, face buried in the crook of his arm.

"Gabe is really asleep," she says, finally.

"I think he's in a lot of pain," says Josie. "I can drive."

Lisi is quick to protest. "It's fine, it's fine," she says. "I can do it. I even got us some new maps of the, um, South . . . Central . . . um, wherever we are in the country right now."

Josie's will to oppose drains dizzily away from him, his swollen eye throbbing.

"Is that good, Josie?" she asks, in a sudden and vulnerable shift that cracks Josie with surprise. "Did I do okay?"

He nods at her fading silhouette, sleep already sucking him back down into an inky unconsciousness.

"It's good, Lisi," he manages. "Thank you."

Lisi knocks on the apartment door but finds it already left open for her. She pushes inside, hitting a breathtaking wall of hot, dry air. Her walk had been bitterly cold, but this was the particular heat of over-worked ovens and radiators in small Manhattan apartments.

"Hello?" she calls, sliding out of her boots and leaving them by the door. "Gabe?"

She turns the corner to find Gabe sitting at his small dinner table, flanked on either side by two empty chairs, fine white candlesticks already lit in the center.

His skin is shiny and taut. His eyeballs seem to sit too heavily in the recessed sockets. Most alarmingly, Gabe is very, very bald, except for the vicious purple semi-circle of scarring that loops over the shell of his right ear and toward the back of his skull. Lisi can see where fresh black stitches bite into the expanse of pale skin.

Gabe lifts an arm with visible effort, sagging as it hovers in the space between them.

"Hey, chickadee," Gabe slurs out of the left side of his mouth. His smile is a lopsided grimace.

She places her serving dish on the table and leans down to meet Gabe's feeble embrace. "Hey!" she chirps, trying hard to keep alarm out of her voice. "Happy Thanksgiving."

Gabe smells sterile. Lisi very immediately feels nauseous. Her eyes scan the apartment for Josie—for his guidance, for his apprehensive over-protectiveness to demand she move away—but Josie is nowhere to be found.

"I made sweet potato casserole," Lisi says, extricating herself carefully. "Can you uh, can you eat it?"

"Psh," Gabe laughs. The exhalation sputters over his drooping lower lip. "'Course I can eat it."

His head rolls momentarily down against his shoulder, as if an invisible thread keeping him upright has been severed. Lisi grips the table and very nearly calls out for help, but Gabe is vertical again just as quickly, though he visibly strains to keep his head raised.

"'Mm gonna"—he pauses to inhale on a noisy rattle—"eat the shit outta it."

Lisi returns a tense little chortle. It's hard to tell if Gabe is present enough to sense her discomfort, if he can suss out her barely concealed revulsion. His eyes seem to scan the room aimlessly, like a person watching scenery pass through a car window.

Mercifully, Josie moves into the room with his hands full of plates and silverware. "You can put your bag and coat in the kitchen," he says to Lisi without looking up from setting the table. "And the turkey's on a platter if you want to bring that back in with you."

"Mhm," Lisi responds tersely. *Just look at me*, Lisi thinks hard, trying to spear the silent thought through the top of Josie's shaggy blond head. He remains silently hunched over their small dinner table, laying out napkins. *Just look at me*, she thinks harder. *Tell me that it's bad and I can figure it out from there.*

But Josie says nothing, so Lisi says nothing, and retreats to kick her coat and backpack under the stools in the kitchen. Josie has prepared a modest smattering of turkey for the three of them, laid out on a nice blue enamel serving platter. All of it feels so incredibly small and stupid and sad. But there's nothing to be done but to take the turkey out from the kitchen, so that is what Lisi does.

She and Josie shuffle about the table, arranging the few plates and dishes as appealingly as possible. Josie pours Lisi a glass of white wine, and none for himself.

"Well, cheers," she says, lifting the glass ceremoniously. Gabe nods jerkily in response.

Josie slides his chair around the table corner until he's sitting just beside Gabe, his own place setting abandoned.

"How was the trip in from Brooklyn?" Josie asks.

"Oh, you know," Lisi says absently, watching Josie fastidiously slice Gabe's turkey into tiny cubes. "Holiday train service."

"Sure," says Josie, sparing only the briefest amount of attention possible that might still be classified as polite. His eyes fix on Gabe. "Here you go," Josie instructs him, lifting a bite to Gabe's mouth.

"Stop'at," Gabe slurs. "I can do it."

Gabe fumbles for his own fork. He covers it with his entire palm, the way a child might, and then closes his fingers around it, deep concentration lining his brow. Josie watches in silence as Gabe scrapes the fork around his plate, not quite spearing anything.

Josie lifts his piece to Gabe's lips again. Gabe eats.

Gabe has found Lisi's eyes and locked onto her gaze, unblinking, but his weary face is unreadable. Their emotions have become inextricable to Lisi; is that shame in Gabe's eyes, or is that what Lisi feels? Is he compelling her to look away, or does Lisi only wish he'd ask her to? She watches his jaw open and close, open and close, very deliberately around the food.

"Okay, big bite this time," Josie says sweetly and raises another forkful to Gabe's lips. Josie talks like Gabe is a child. Lisi resents that for no real, sensible reason other than that she can actually remember Gabe as a child, and he was never this helpless. With five years between them, he was always easily idolized, but the chasm of experience between them was never too wide. He shepherded her into every new and exciting brush with maturity: the traded mixtapes burned onto unlabeled CD-Rs, the electric camaraderie in feeling too big and too different for their hometown, the downtown crowd of bona fide avant-garde artists Lisi would have never met without Gabe's introductions.

Josie dabs a napkin at Gabe's chin. Gabe's head bobs again on his thin neck—going fully slack, and then his head rolls back to attention—and Lisi is finally free of his stare.

"Um, excuse me," Lisi says, pushing her chair away from the table. She realizes she needs an excuse, so she reaches for her wine glass. She retreats to the privacy of the kitchen as quickly as she can.

She feels just as trapped in the tiny apartment kitchen, wedged between the radiating heat of the still-warm oven and the noisy refrigerator. Lisi has no idea what it will look like when Gabe is sicker. She doesn't know if this is even close to the worst of it. She doesn't know what life without Gabe is like; she has never known it. It is, in the truest meaning of the word, unimaginable. Her brain skips like a broken record trying to comprehend any part of it.

"You asked," Josie says from behind her, his voice uncommonly low and full of gravel.

Lisi curses and snaps around. "You scared me," she hisses.

He steps closer, undeterred. "You asked. You *insisted*."

"What?" Lisi splutters.

"You said we should do Thanksgiving together."

"Okay," Lisi says. Her eyes flit desperately toward the dining room, but Gabe seems not to have even noticed they're missing.

"He told you he was having surgery. You still wanted to come. So I cooked, and Gabe put on clothes, and *this*"—Josie gesticulates sharply behind him, and then back at Lisi with markedly less energy, as though he were a rapidly deflating balloon—"is what Thanksgiving looks like."

Lisi refuses to meet his eyes; instead, she studies the glass of wine clutched in her hand. Josie had always been foreign to her: demure and serious and laconic. This Josie is especially uncanny. She has never seen him behave with any sort of aggression. It fills her with both unease and a measure of embarrassment, like watching a teacher lose their temper.

"And you're making it very clear that you don't like it."

"Oh, and I'm sure you love it," Lisi sneers, with a waggle of her fingers at stalwart, unflappable little Josie, there guarding the doorway, penning her in.

The regret is instant and collides into the back of her skull like a brick.

"Sorry. Fuck." She paces around herself in a tight, captive circle. "I don't—I just mean it's really weird. It's all so fucking weird."

She sucks in hard through her teeth and holds her breath until it begins to ache in her chest. Josie looks almost embarrassed by her outburst, which is so much worse than his disdain.

"He's sick, Lisi," he says in his infuriatingly even way, as though it were some simple, easy instruction she alone—bafflingly—could not comprehend. "He can't perform for you."

"I didn't say—" Lisi stammers. "That is *not* what I'm saying. I just wanted to be with him. Gabe is my favorite person."

Josie huffs sharply and drops his head into his palms, pressing the heels of his hands into his eyes. He stands there like that for an interminable, silent moment, long enough for Lisi to begin composing an apology. It is only as Josie inhales, his face rising, that Lisi realizes he's laughing. His bent elbows frame an infuriating smile.

"Your favorite person," Josie repeats, breathless with laughter. He wipes his wrist across his wet eyes as the hysteria simmers away. "Then why are you hiding in the kitchen?"

Lisi swallows hard. "I'm not hiding. I was getting more wine."

"I see," he answers slyly. His eyes are settled on her still-empty wine glass.

She turns away, itchy with the sensation of being patronized, and snatches the bottle of white wine off the counter. Her hands are trembling so badly that she overfills her glass to a ridiculous degree.

She can feel Josie's eyes boring into the back of her neck. There's a part of herself that dares to outlast him, to dig her heels in and simply wait for him to leave her alone, so that he won't see the stupid, over-poured glass and her shaking shoulders and the glassiness of unshed tears in her eyes. Instead she buckles, as she often does, desperate for a mote of Josie's sympathy.

"You're making me feel bad for reacting," she says. "Like, I'm seeing what I'm seeing, and I'm having a response, and I'm the crazy one? Nobody's talking about how bad it is!"

"He knows it's bad," Josie answers flatly. "Why should we make him talk about it?"

"That's not what I mean," Lisi deflects, turning to face him, though she isn't entirely sure what the crux of her argument is anymore. She reaches for whatever she can, whatever feelings words can encompass. "I'm just not . . . not used to it like you are."

Josie's face goes hard. "I am not used to it," he says. "I am just here."

"And *I'd* be here more if you weren't so obsessed with shutting me out!" she protests. Simmering beneath her rage is a profound knowledge that her distance from Gabe was entirely of her own doing. But it is too easy to hate Josie for his quietness and his mothering and the way he is so easily imagined in the role of arbiter, meting out who poor Gabe is allowed to see or what he is allowed to do. "Like, if I knew more, then I wouldn't be freaking out so much. But you don't trust me, and you don't even know me, and I'm your *family*—"

"Lisi," he interrupts coolly, "what's my last name?"

Lisi looks away. The faucet is dripping into a dirty pot left in the sink. The continuous *plink-plink-plink* is the only sound, save for Lisi's labored breathing.

"I don't know," she croaks, anger throttling her throat closed. "You don't have a Facebook."

Josie snatches the wine glass out of her hand and dumps it into the kitchen sink. Lisi gasps in shock, at the humiliation, at the quick decisiveness of Josie's actions.

"If you can't convince Gabe you want to be here, and that you want to see him as much as he wants to see you, then you need to find an excuse to leave."

Josie had said exactly what she both wanted and hated to hear. He knew it as well as she did: she couldn't make it through the night. But only he was brave enough to suggest it.

"What do I say?" she rasps, thumbing a tear from the corner of her eye and hoping Josie does not notice.

"You act, don't you? You can think of something."

Lisi feels sick and strangled, like she'd swallowed liquid metal, quickly hardening in her esophagus. She grabs her coat and shrugs it on, furious at Josie, and at Gabe for being so sick and ugly, and at herself for merely having the capacity to harbor that thought.

She brushes past Josie into the dining room and drops a quick kiss on Gabe's head. The skin there is dry and thin as paper. "I'm so sorry," she says, talking faster than her brain can manage sensible thought. "If it wasn't an emergency, I wouldn't. You know? So I'm gonna. Got to. I'm so sorry. Happy holiday!"

Lisi stumbles down the three narrow flights of stairs and out onto the street, gulping in the frigid nighttime air like a drowned man. Tears blur the streetlamps and passing headlights into long smears. More by memory than sight, Lisi walks a long and silent avenue down to a nearby bar Gabe used to like.

"Alone on the holiday, huh?" the bartender asks. Something about his tone keeps the question from feeling mean. Lisi watches him un-stack clean glasses. He looks healthy or maybe just young, but either way it is a relief.

"Mm-hmm," answers Lisi. His eyes linger on her as she shrugs her jacket off. Even Lisi isn't sure if it's a lie. She *is* alone. She does not know at that moment in time that next Thanksgiving would pass without an invitation from Gabe and Josie, or that she wouldn't again be in a room with the both of them until the world was ending.

What she does know is she wants to get sick-drunk, obliterated, blackout, so when she wakes up tomorrow feeling awful about herself, she can have an excuse.

EIGHTEEN DAYS

"What time is it?" Gabe croaks from the back seat.

"Gabe!" Lisi and Josie chirp in unison. Josie folds down his wrinkled roadmap and rushes to click off the droning radio. Gabe only barely catches the words "scarcity of resources."

"I'm so glad you're awake," says Lisi, just as Josie answers, "It's nearly two."

Gabe blinks at the roof of the car, struggling to push himself up onto his elbows, blinking owlishly into the strong, midday sunlight. His thighs are suctioned to the leather seat. "My fucking pants . . ."

"Oh, I have them," Lisi assures him. "They're in the trunk. Do you want me to pull over? I think we should pull over. That'd be good for us."

She carefully slows as they veer off the highway, over the flat and unfenced shoulder of the road, and beyond that onto a stretch of patchy grass with a sparse forest behind. They had stayed south enough to avoid St. Louis and had fortuitously found themselves on empty roads, dipping in and out of verdancy.

Lisi pulls over beneath a short, pitted tree bleached from the sun. "You need help?" she asks, craning over her shoulder toward Gabe in the back seat.

"I'm fine, I'm fine," he grouses. "Best I've ever felt."

Lisi pops the trunk, then excuses herself to walk and relieve herself. Gabe watches as she traipses along the uneven tree line with her cell phone raised above her head, still angling for pockets of service.

Despite a lingering dizziness and a parched mouth, Gabe has largely regained his faculties, and steps into his jeans without assistance. He watches as Josie sidles stiffly out of the passenger seat and paces away to stand in a slat of sunlight, bouncing as he shifts weight between his swollen feet.

"Need a stretch?" Gabe asks. Josie stays turned toward the road but shakes his head. There, standing still in the middle of the dust, Josie looks like an abandoned lamppost—unbending and worn, left behind as new roads had diverged.

"I'm fine. Lisi and I stopped this morning," Josie answers. "But you must be hungry."

Gabe shrugs. "I can't tell. That medicine always makes me feel like I swallowed a basketball."

"Please trust me. You're hungry." Josie gestures behind him without turning toward the car. "There are almonds in the back seat."

Gabe picks at a sun-warmed bag of almonds while Josie paces up and down the tire tracks they'd left in the dust, his eyes never leaving the parallel road.

"Babe," Gabe appeals, "what are you looking for?"

Josie doesn't answer. He had been singularly focused as they traveled, but this taciturn, grave mood—this seemingly calculated estrangement—is not like him. Gabe lopes behind him in brisk strides.

"Jo," he calls out, clapping his hand onto one of Josie's tensed shoulders. Josie must've been even more preoccupied than Gabe anticipated, because Josie whips to face him with such alarm that Gabe's confusion immediately morphs into apologetic concern.

But the apology dies on his lips, Gabe left gawping, dumbstruck. "Your *face*," he says.

"Is it bad?" Josie asks, thumbing at the mottled purple beneath his eye. "I can still see out of it."

"I don't remember what happened. Did you get hit?"

"You don't remember," says Josie, without the shape and lift of a question.

"There was a man," Gabe answers, hoping not to seem too obtuse. He is reticent to say much more and risk upsetting Josie further.

Josie nods stiffly. "Well," he concludes with a vague turn of his wrist between them, as if that motion detailed anything left unexplained. "We're all right and that's all you need to know."

In that moment, Gabe feels he can spy the true Josie fumbling behind the façade of resilience, and as that Josie shifts back into focus, Gabe is overcome with fondness. *How like him*, Gabe thinks warmly. *Unwilling to alarm anyone. Josie will fix it, like he always does.* Gabe tuts and angles over him, one hand cupping Josie's neck, the other reaching to brush his fingers through Josie's matted hair.

"Poor baby," Gabe croons. "I didn't protect you."

Josie ducks his chin and twists out of the hutch of Gabe's arms. He stalks away, a furious, compact little thing, hands shoved deep into both pockets, shoulders bunched at the level of his ears.

"Josie!" Gabe calls after him, hustling to intercept Josie before he can go too far. "Jo, Jo, I'm sorry. I wasn't teasing. I swear."

Josie halts by the road. "I know you weren't," he answers, still faced away.

"I didn't actually think—" Gabe begins but thinks better of trying to defend his approach. "You know I trust you. Right?"

He watches Josie deflate, tense shoulders dropping, followed by his loose and heavy hands. He is all at once limp, like an animal surrendering in the jaws of something much larger. He turns back around, his tangled hair hanging over his eyes, a shadow disguising the worst of his injury.

"I'm so ashamed," Josie says, in a hollow monotone. "Last night nearly got us killed."

"Jo," Gabe says, "that was really unlucky."

"No. *That* was the world," Josie counters. "What we've been is lucky. Not the other way around."

When Lisi returns from her walk, Josie is back behind the wheel, Gabe up front, like nothing has happened.

"It was so *dark* in that office," Gabe grouses. "You really didn't notice?"

Josie shrugs. "I suppose I did."

Gabe removes his denim jacket. "I could never work in an office like that," he says. "But then again I could never work in an office." He flicks his jacket onto the coat hook in the front hall and saunters off into the bedroom.

Josie plods behind him, so exhausted that it takes conscious effort to lift his feet into full steps. The three hours they just spent with the attorney—drafting a living will for Gabe, negotiating Josie's responsibilities as healthcare proxy—drained him to the marrow. They would have to return sometime before Gabe's upcoming surgery to draw up a last will and testament. Gabe had always been flippant about the matter ("What do I have to leave behind? And who would I give it to but you?"), but he was historically glib about these sorts of things, these looming legal matters all tied to his fate. It depresses Josie in a way he is too embarrassed to express, loathe to ask Gabe to take his own impending death more seriously.

"Gabe," Josie calls after him. "Can I ask you something? The attorney—it was brought up, but we changed the subject . . ."

"'Course," says Gabe, shucking his shirt and tossing it onto the bed. He sits on the edge, beginning his nightly routine of stretching.

"Whatever your answer is, I'll make sure it's respected," Josie says. "I mean, I'll take it seriously."

Gabe cranes to look up at Josie from his bent-backed position, the two bare mountains of his shoulder blades protruding sharply out of his underweight frame. His hair has started to grow back, fuzzy and uneven, and Josie cannot shake the image of him as some baby bird, pop-eyed and gawkish.

Josie continues. "If. If it really. . . came down to it. Should I invite your parents?"

"Where?"

"To a funeral."

Gabe's expression hardens for the briefest moment, eyes flashing with something hot and vicious but quickly battled back. He shrugs. "Whatever you wanna do, Jo," he answers coolly, rolling flat on his back to stretch out his hips. One hand rises in the air, gesturing broadly. "I don't care."

Josie steps closer to the bed, willing Gabe to look at him. "I'm sorry, but you have to care. You can't make these decisions once . . ."

"Once I'm dead?" Gabe concludes for him, snapping upright. "How can I *begin* to care about shit that's gonna happen after I'm dead?"

"I shouldn't have said anything. It's not healthy for us to be talking like this at home," Josie warns, clamping down on the unruly tangle of his emotions. "We can discuss this with the lawyers."

Gabe barks one short, brittle laugh of disbelief. "Why discuss it at all? Fuck having a funeral! You'll be the one stuck paying for it."

"It's not inappropriate for your colleagues to want to come and pay respects."

Gabe springs to his feet, briefly looming over Josie before he stalks to the opposite end of their tiny bedroom, throwing his hands above his head. "To *who*? I'm already dead!"

"*For* you," Josie corrects him. "In your honor."

Gabe rolls his eyes. "Yeah, I really need the dance faculty at the New School to come rend their garments for me," he mocks, pulling at his face theatrically. "Boo hoo hoo, now we need to find another adjunct."

Josie staggers back onto the bed, elbows digging into his thighs, knuckles pressed into his eye sockets hard enough to stymie his tears. Josie's brain untethers in a familiar and practiced way, white whorls of light filling his vision, drifting into sightlessness.

"Jo," he hears Gabe say. Sound has gone fuzzy. Gabe sounds like a television. "I know you think that because you love me, everyone must love me. But that's not what's going to happen. It'll be just you and Lisi, sitting alone with a cheese plate."

Gabe is wrong, of course. Josie knows that. Gabe knows, even in the heat of the moment. But apathy is the best disguise, the most palatable way to excise the terror, and the rage against the unfairness of it all. Grief is a sun, impossible to ignore but debilitating to look at for too long. Instead, Gabe could conjure some glib comment, something dismissive and wry and reactionary. And Josie could get riled up. Together, they'd traverse the acceptable peaks and valleys: the tiff, the apology at the end, maybe even a tearful kiss, and a promise of learning something. And the next day they could wake up and do it all again.

But the dread. The deep, existential dread. It was wringing them both dry.

Josie hears Gabe's footsteps on the carpet as he approaches.

"I've upset you."

"Yes," chokes Josie.

"Well, I'm sorry for that," Gabe offers, free of anything insincere or sardonic. He rests his hand on Josie's hunched shoulders. "Will you look at me so I can apologize?"

Josie lifts his head. His cheeks are wet, despite his best efforts.

"I'm sorry, Jo." Gabe extends his hand and pulls Josie to his feet. "I'm not making this any easier for you."

"You don't have to be sorry," Josie mumbles, finding his way into Gabe's arms, mostly thankful that it seems the fuel has run out on their argument. He presses his cheek into Gabe's sternum, and Gabe squeezes back.

"I wouldn't have believed you if you told me dying came with apologizing to so many people," Gabe chuckles.

"You're not dying," Josie protests, muffled against Gabe's skin. If Gabe hears him, he does not respond. Josie doesn't have the fortitude to repeat it.

In bed, Josie winds himself around Gabe. For years, Josie happily slotted under Gabe's chin, his feet tucked under Gabe's warm calves as they plodded lazily into sleep together. But Gabe is always cold now. Josie cannot remember the first night their positions reversed, but at some point he had moved to hold Gabe's trembling ribs against his chest, his warm stomach pillowing Gabe's lower back, and now each day ended with a return to that familiar position.

"Josie?" says Gabe into the darkness.

"Mm?"

"I really am sorry that I'm dying."

Josie feels his heart dive into his stomach. "We don't know that yet," he says. "We're still trying."

"Yeah," Gabe says after a significant silence. "You're right. Night, Jo."

Josie lies awake, his face pressed into the back of Gabe's neck. Treatment has somehow made Gabe's skin smell different. But sometimes, on his well-worn clothes, the Gabe he remembers lingers stubbornly. Josie drinks it in gratefully and exhales the tension and discomfort of arguing.

Josie knows Gabe was correct about one thing, whether it was a premeditated moment of clarity or something expressed thoughtlessly in the heat of the moment.

There would be mourners: friends and colleagues and likely even family, despite Gabe's assuredness otherwise. They would linger for hours or pass through for a moment, cry or stay heroically stoic, perhaps offer to stay and help clean up or get Josie home.

But Gabe was right. At the end, after all of that came and went, it would be just Josie and Lisi. Lisi and Josie. Carrying on.

FOURTEEN DAYS

The landscape changes dramatically partway through Oklahoma, green prairie peeling back into expanses of rock and sand, landscape dotted by dry, twisted trees. The stretches between any hints of civilization have become few and far between. At first there is a sense of relief, their incident at the motel having left them shaken and too afraid to sleep anywhere but the car.

The first three nights of travel through this landscape, completely alone on the road save for the occasional news broadcast and the snatches of music that waft in and out, are near carefree. But as the gas in the tank dwindles, the mood sours, and long, lonely stretches of miles begin to feel more like a challenge than a blessing.

They stop somewhere in New Mexico, not far from the border of Arizona, pulling off the highway and secreting the car off-road in a tall thicket of dry brush. The rock formations around them loom large, casting strange, almost human-shaped shadows that creep across the landscape as the sun sets.

They fall into their new routine: shoes removed, chairs reclined, the overhead lights clicked off, with the car keys and Lisi's little can of mace resting on the console ready for use at any moment. Lisi curls up in the back seat facing away from the windshield. Josie watches her shoulders rise and fall evenly, signaling sleep.

"Gabe?" Josie whispers, settling on his side in the driver's seat to face him.

Gabe has splayed as wide as he can in the reclined passenger seat, shielding his eyes in the crook of his elbow. His wrist twitches, and then he unfurls, gracefully, like a leaf peeling back from a bud.

"Jo?" he rasps. "Did you say something?"

"I woke you," Josie frets. "I'm sorry, go back to sleep."

Gabe shifts, turning toward him, blinking as he strains to see Josie in the rapidly dimming light. His pupils are blown wide and black in a way that quite nearly recalls Gabe in moments of untrammeled passion. Josie quickly spurs those thoughts away.

"I'm not asleep," says Gabe. "Tell me."

Josie sucks in a breath through his teeth and has to will himself to swallow it down, like a mouthful of something bitter. "My eye hurts," he answers at length. "That's all."

"Jo," Gabe says, in a tone expertly sharpened from years of whittling at Josie.

Josie plans his words diplomatically. "We shouldn't go out of our way. It's stupid to do it."

"What's that?"

"Go out of our way to see the Grand Canyon. We can't spare the gas." Then Josie shrugs, anticipating Gabe's protestations. "I won't be upset."

Gabe sits upright. "I will be," he says.

Josie shrinks under his unblinking scrutiny, Gabe straight-backed and tall while Josie presses his cheek further into the upholstered car seat, desperate to dissolve into it.

"The *one* thing you wanted to see, Jo," he expounds, his voice climbing urgently out of a whisper. Josie winces and presses his finger against his own lips pleadingly, trying to deter Gabe without raising his own voice. "It's why we left New York!"

"We left to take Lisi to Sacramento."

"I don't give a shit about Sacramento," says Gabe. "I don't. I really don't, Josie, and you know that."

Josie presses his knuckles into his eyes. Gabe gives him too much credit for knowing what he, or anyone, wanted. Josie accepted good things as a sign not to squeeze for more and misfortune as a sign he'd asked for too much.

"We left so we could travel together. So you could see things!"

"If we go that way, we won't make it to Sacramento," Josie protests. "Don't you see how she—" Josie can't think of the words so he demonstrates, holding his clenched hand aloft in the air between them and swinging it around, mimicking Lisi fishing for cell phone reception. "—with her cell phone? Every minute of every day. Lisi will be heartbroken."

"You're not our chauffeur," Gabe snaps. "You're my fucking boyfriend."

Lisi exhales noisily behind them but does not wake. They sit in tense silence, staring at each other but unsure how to proceed. Gabe bows under the pressure first, flattening his hand very solemnly over his heart.

"I'm sorry, Jo," he says. "I'm not mad at you."

"Feels like it."

"I'm not," he repeats. "I feel . . ." Gabe goes quiet, seemingly trying to summon the correct words. "I feel a responsibility," he manages, "to make sure you're part of it. Part of the End. We can share it, now. Now that I'm not . . ."

Gabe trails off, but his meaning is understood. He turns onto his side to face Josie, sinking down in his seat so that their faces are level.

"There is a Josie in here," Gabe says, tapping his finger against Josie's temple, "who is a complete stranger to me."

It nearly makes Josie laugh. Not because it is untrue, but because it is too vast to untangle. Josie had shied away from it for years. There is so much that Josie swore to himself he would tell Gabe before he lost him, but with mutual destruction assured and so few days left, the desire had only waned, replaced by the urge to do nothing but please Gabe for as long as he could.

"C'mon. Let me inside," Gabe needles, perhaps just for Josie's reaction, which traverses shock and hunger and abashment in great, roiling waves. Gabe had a delicious way of being selfish even in his selflessness, which made Josie feel intensely important and cherished, like Josie was something Gabe could not bear to share with the rest of the world.

It was that quality that attracted people to Gabe; the way his inner life seemed so enviably assured and robust, how his attention was so complete and nourishing. Josie had already let Gabe in more than any other living person, and every admission had been met with genuine delight. That Josie knew how to milk a cow. That he kept his social security card in an Altoids box but did not own a passport. That he worked the overnight shift at the GAP in Times Square all through college because he did not want to speak to customers, but he enjoyed folding clothes. But there came a limit, Josie reasoned. There was always a limit.

Gabe yawns, settling back into a sprawled position that seems nearly, and against all odds, comfortable. "You make me absolutely crazy," he drawls. "I love you."

Josie doesn't sleep well, and so begins the approach to the Grand Canyon through the earliest hours of the morning, Lisi and Gabe still dozing. The drive takes them through the national forest and up into the park proper. Lisi and Gabe wake as the sun licks a syrupy pink through the car windows, refracting off the red, red rocks surrounding them. Gabe takes Josie's free hand and squeezes it.

Despite the early hour, they're not alone as they approach the parking areas around the South Rim. Some have set up tents or appear to be living out of their cars. Josie figures he's not alone in wanting to see it before he dies; there were worse places to camp out until the End comes.

From the parking lot, Josie cannot discern much. The unobstructed sky is a hazy lilac, dotted with candy-colored clouds. There's a chill in the air not yet dispelled by the rising sun.

Lisi takes charge, which Josie is grateful for, following signs that wind them up narrow, rocky trails toward designated vistas. He hangs behind, his hand in Gabe's, feeling strangely uneasy.

Josie has trouble with expectations—holding his own and those required of him. He's long had a habit of detaching from his own desires with unthinking ease. Nearly six years ago, near the very start of their relationship, Gabe had managed to suss out Josie's birthday without asking, and purchased Josie a gorgeous, lavish set of enamel cookware. It was not merely a gift—gifts were rarely just gifts when they came from Gabe—it was a profession of love in his usual way: exorbitant, unrestrained, unembarrassed. Josie had to ask Gabe to look away while he unwrapped everything, too afraid that his reaction wouldn't measure up to Gabe's expectation.

Now more than halfway across the country, at the one destination Josie had wanted to see before the end, he feels nothing but guilt. He can sharply imagine Gabe and Lisi studying his blank expression, perceiving nothing but ungratefulness there, weighing if he liked it enough to bother wasting their precious little time.

Then they crest a rising hill, greeted by the vision of the ground split open before them. Rock, water, vegetation, all painted by the sun in colors Josie doesn't possess language for. He darts ahead to the very edge, breathless, his anxiety overwhelmed by a feeling of bone-deep awe.

"What do you think, Josie?" Lisi chirps, jostling his shoulder convivially.

He feels unable to comprehend it, all of its individual parts nearly too large and too magnificent to understand. The immense sky is clear and unobstructed, the red rocks seemingly alive, lit from within. The scope so massive, and Josie so small. He nearly swoons, suddenly quite afraid of the ledge.

"I need to sit down," he says, and so he does, right where he'd been standing. Gabe and Lisi perch behind him, the sound of their conversation dampened by the rhythmic, ocean-like sweeping of wind through the canyon.

Josie sits for a long time as the sun begins to arc up toward its zenith, casting long, shifting shadows across the shimmering cliffs and gullies. The thunder of faraway water is hypnotic. Josie has never seen anything like it, and is almost afraid to see much more. There are only thirteen remaining days. Once they drive away, Sacramento their final destination, he will never be able to return. He fears becoming greedy for it, enamored by the idea of just a little more time. Gabe was already the great beauty of his life, and Josie had lived every day for the past three taxing years terrified of their parting, bargaining for more.

"Babe," Gabe says, and Josie looks up, noticing that at some point Gabe and Lisi must have gotten up and walked around without him, allowing him to sit and experience his seismic thoughts in private. Josie can feel stiffness in his joints and the tightness of a sunburn across the bridge of his nose.

"It's past noon," Gabe continues, and Josie realizes he is correct. The sun is high and hot above them.

"Oh," says Josie, his voice weak from disuse. "I'm sorry."

"Do you want to do something else before we leave?"

"No," says Josie.

"We can hike a little along the rim," Lisi pipes up. "We don't have to go far."

"No, thank you," Josie answers, rising to his feet.

"Pretty different from Ohio, huh?" Lisi teases sweetly. Josie supposes she has remembered some details about him, after all.

Gabe runs his hand up and down Josie's bare arm, sun-warmed and freckled. "Are you okay?" he asks. "Do you need something?"

"Thank you for taking me here," Josie says.

"*You* took us," Gabe says, laughing. "Don't give me credit."

Josie shakes his head. He can't explain. Instead, he takes one photo on his phone and heads back down the trail with Gabe and Lisi in tow.

"What did you think?" Lisi asks when they arrive at the car. Josie is devoid of words, but her excitement is so genuine, so guileless and deeply felt. He is surprised that her full attention, like Gabe's, is a warm and bolstering thing.

"It was really good," Josie says. "I liked it."

And in saying it, his lip begins to quiver, and he dissolves into tears.

FIFTEEN YEARS, ONE MONTH, AND SEVEN DAYS

There's a nasty rumor going around about Josiah. Josiah was caught trying to pay a man to drive him out of town. The man was a contractor, they say. He drove in from Pennsylvania to install new fire sprinklers in the local grocery store, and Josiah offered him all of the cash in his wallet to take him away, as far as he was willing to travel. There's a version of this rumor where Josiah makes it as far as the state line before his father chases him down, but there are other people who know that can't be true since Mister Rempel can't drive, even if it does make for an exciting story.

His eldest sister, Sue, cast herself across the couch and wept when she first heard the news, certain the Bohn family would no longer allow Eli to propose to her, now that the Rempels were so outwardly troubled. Even little Lottie seems wracked with guilt, fearful to be seen escorted home from school by wayward Josiah, yet thankful that he is still willing to carry her up the big hill. No one can discern the truth of the rumor or from where it had originated, but everyone knows it. Josiah and the strange man. Josiah running off.

What is true is that the Rempel family sits in the very first pew every Sunday now, with Josiah right there on the aisle, so that everyone can see him. So that he can greet everyone as they enter and exit, hello Missus Frey, hello to the family of Schrocks, hello Mister Edigers. So that everyone can see that he is a good boy, from a good family, and anything you may hear to the contrary is nothing more than foolishness. Watch Josiah's mouth move, watch how he knows every word to every prayer and hymn. His voice—thin and high—can be heard above the broad, even voice of the congregation. Josiah is exemplary. Josiah follows the teachings of the sermons. Josiah is the only boy in the Rempel family, and he takes that responsibility seriously, with humbleness and civility.

What is true is that Josiah liked to sit in the back of the congregation before he was moved up front. There are large wooden ceiling fans that paddle the hot air about in great, lazy churns. Etta would admonish him and say he was only so warm because he'd let himself get fat. She did not know there was a lick of fire in his stomach as his eyes grazed over the pale arch of other boys' necks, bent in prayer.

What is true is that Josiah used to fear that God was immense, and everywhere, and displeased with him. That is how the impassioned ministers spoke about God. But recently Josiah was beginning to fear that perhaps God was very small, and very far away, and intensely disinterested in Josiah's life.

No one knows what Josiah said to that man, that contractor from Pennsylvania. Not even God. God's left Josiah to fend for himself.

THIRTEEN DAYS

Against Josie's instincts, they circle toward Las Vegas to search for gas while there's still daylight. They have avoided cities so thoroughly that it is hard not to catastrophize the state civilization might be in. But even if scraped clean or left in chaos, the dregs of something monumental seem like a better option than taking a risk along the back roads and desert.

The interstate spits them out along the outskirts of downtown. In the darkening late afternoon, they can see the bright lights of the Strip a few miles ahead, neon and promising.

But as the roadsides become increasingly lined with attractions, the litters of strangers amass.

Gabe curses under his breath, angling forward to survey the scene through the windshield. The road ahead is swarmed with people mingling blithely in the street, so many that their car won't be able to pass. Josie's heart catches in his throat, his mind assailed with images of desperation, robbery, violence. They'd been lucky escaping the first time, and that was against the threat of only one man.

Josie slows, already scanning for the fastest exits, debating if he can jump the curb and drive around the herd. But as they approach, the crowd coming into focus, it's apparent there is very little sense of desperation at all.

People stand huddled, many with drinks in hand, pressed close and chattering away. The mood is giddy, inebriated—a bobbing, happy mass. They give the approaching car no mind, not even stepping out of the way, now so close that Josie can hear their tittering conversations through the window.

"Jesus," Lisi huffs under her breath. "It's like they don't even see us!"

The crowd appears to have largely spilled out of a small roadside chapel, painted in cutesy pastels. But beside that chapel, beneath a comically grand white trellis, are two gas pumps.

They needn't say anything, all eyes settling on it at once.

Josie maneuvers off the road at a crawling pace, having to wait for crowds to clear in order to proceed. They pull near and bound out of the car, surrounding the strange pumps to inspect. They're somewhat old fashioned, but seem to be in polished, pristine condition.

"Oh my god," Lisi squawks, yanking wildly at the fuel nozzle, which is shellacked to the rest of the pump. "They're props. They're like . . . 1950s nostalgia bullshit!"

"No," gasps Gabe, giving the pump closest to him a jerk for good measure. It doesn't budge, same as Lisi's hadn't.

Josie scrubs his hands hard over his face. "Why would they do such a stupid thing?" he says. "Oh, I hate stupid things."

"Someone around here has to know," Gabe appeals, leaning over the hood of the car toward Josie, "has to have some idea of what's *real* around here. Right?"

Josie peeks over his fingers with a wilting, weary expression. "I don't want to talk to them," he grouses. "They're all drunk."

"I'll talk," says Gabe, extending his hand. "Trust me. You trust me, don't you?"

Huffing, Josie takes his hand. He fights very hard not to roll his eyes as he turns and follows Gabe inside.

Inside the chapel, the mood is equally boisterous. They enter to the sound of cheering. Two people are clasped together on a small, raised altar, kissing in a way Josie would describe as *violently.*

"Jesus," mutters Lisi, surveying the scene. In the wake of the celebratory kiss, champagne bottles are popped, and new couplings find each other, indulging in long, impassioned embraces.

"I'm leaving if clothes start coming off," Lisi quips, leaning over Josie's shoulder. But she is right. It's a crowd full of pleasure seekers, by the purest definition. Josie recalls the crowds that had overtaken the abandoned motels, but this lacks the precarious feeling of anarchy.

On the altar behind the couple, serenely presiding over the hullabaloo, is a man in a powder-blue suit, dabbing at his eyes with a handkerchief that he then re-rolls and slides into his breast pocket.

"One more cheer for the new bride and groom," he announces to the room, who all manage to disentangle themselves from their current partner to applaud or whoop in encouragement. "Whoever's next, why don't you step on down to the altar now?"

It is apparent to Josie that this man is some semblance of a leader, and the most likely to make any meaning out of the pandemonium. Gabe seems to catch the same inclination, nudging Josie as he mutters, "This guy knows, if anyone does."

Josie cannot mask his discomfort, craning back around to spot the exit, which has been obstructed by swooning revelers. But before he can manage to protest, Gabe has begun to press forward through the crowd. Josie and Lisi trail behind him in the wake that he clears. As Gabe approaches the minister, he throws up his hand in a friendly salute, which the man giddily returns.

"Do we know each other?" the man asks. "You have a familiar look about you."

"Don't think so," Gabe deflects with a wide, toothy smile. Gabe pushes his hands into his front pockets, mirroring the man's posture. "We just saw such a friendly looking crowd and hoped you might be able to help us."

Gabe's charm is so genuine, so expert, that Josie catches himself gaping. Gabe even seems to match the man's lilting, easy drawl. It was a given that Gabe was a performer, but catching it in a new context is somehow still staggering.

"Wyatt," the man introduces himself, shaking Gabe's hand firm-ly. Wyatt looks over Gabe's shoulder toward Lisi and Josie, hovering politely behind.

"Say no more. You've shepherded in a lovely young couple this afternoon. Would you like to get married?" asks Wyatt. "You'd be my seventh couple today."

"Oh, god," Lisi gasps, springing away from Josie.

Josie steps forward, clasping Gabe's arm protectively.

"This is my boyfriend," Gabe says.

"Ah! Blessings to the lovely couple!" Wyatt rhapsodizes. "Offer still stands."

Josie flushes red. "We aren't joking," Josie says.

Wyatt quite nearly looks offended, his lower lip pouting over the shelf of his blond beard. "Neither am I," he answers. "My humble duty is to make sure we all meet the End how we always dreamed we might. Not many more days left now. Wanna die married?"

Gabe jostles Josie's shoulder.

Josie looks up at him, flabbergasted. "Gabe, the *gas*?" he presses from behind gritted teeth.

"I'll ask," Gabe assures him in a whisper before snapping back toward Wyatt with enthusiasm.

"What would we need?" Gabe answers Wyatt, blissfully unde-terred. "Do we need witnesses? I guess we have Lisi."

Lisi springs forward, elated. "I'll be a witness!"

"We don't have any documentation," says Josie.

Wyatt furrows his brow. "Documentation?"

"Like birth certificates?"

Wyatt laughs and claps Josie hard on the shoulder. "Kid. You don't have papers? Neither do I. I'm not a minister."

"Sorry," Lisi splutters, cutting in. "You're not?"

"*Today* I am!" Wyatt counters gleefully. He extends his arms wide. "These people don't seem to notice the difference."

Josie effectively edges his way in front of Gabe to face him. He lowers his voice, very aware of not just Wyatt's eyes on them, but the rest of the motley congregation. "We don't have to do this," says Josie.

Gabe's eyebrows raise. "You don't want to marry me?"

Josie flushes bright red. "Oh, Gabe," he says, "It's not that. Just look at all these . . ."

Josie doesn't finish that sentence, nor does he need to. The atmosphere is sloppy and strange, brimming with happiness that threatens to teeter into an orgiastic sort of chaos. Josie is shy in even the most mundane of circumstances; the attention of so many strangers feels hot against his neck like a sunburn. It makes his knees weak.

Gabe's eyes drag over the crowd of revelers. "I don't care about these people," Gabe declares at length. "I'm not going to remember them."

Josie looks to Lisi, hands clasped beneath her chin in utter delight, and back to Gabe, bright-eyed and gravely serious.

"I've always wanted to marry you," Gabe says.

"Gabe," Josie replies, feeling the sudden pinprick of tears in his eyes. He feels incapable of raising his voice out of a hoarse whisper, every word like the hazy rasp of snow underfoot. "Of course I want to be married to you."

Gabe's tongue darts quickly over his bottom lip, a bright and wild smile blossoming on his face. "Say it again."

Josie clears his throat. "I want to be married to you."

Gabe's hand is suddenly at the back of Josie's head, and he is bending down to kiss him hard. The force leans Josie back so that he has to fist his hands in Gabe's shirt to stay upright. The swell of noise around them is unignorable, but Gabe seems undeterred. Perhaps the attention even encourages him.

"Ah, stop, you're skipping the middle part!" Wyatt insists, now atop his pulpit. Gabe releases Josie, whose lips feel swollen and cheeks flushed from a confusing muddle of embarrassment and arousal. They turn toward the man under his baby blue trellis full of faded paper flowers. The establishment had quite clearly seen better days and yet felt as full of uncomplicated happiness as any room ever could.

"What's your name?" Wyatt asks, pointing one long finger at Gabe.

"Me? Gabe."

"Full name!"

"Ah," Gabe laughs. "Sorry. Gabriel Fish."

"Do you, Gabriel Fish," the man booms, clearly delighting in his self-aggrandizing importance, "take . . ." His voice quiets conspiratorially. "And your name?" he asks, lowering his eyes to Josie.

"Josie Rempel."

"Take Josie Rempel," Wyatt continues in his billowing, operatic tone, "to be your lawfully wedded husband?"

"I do," says Gabe.

"And uh, the same to you?" he asks of Josie.

Josie has to bite back his laughter at the casual sloppiness of the ceremony in comparison to his memories of long, intensely religious services, the unyielding backbone of tradition.

"I do," says Josie, regardless.

"Do you have rings to exchange?" Wyatt asks.

Gabe has clasped Josie's hands in his own, palm to palm, unwilling to let go. "We do not," Gabe titters, eyes alight, as if barely containing a bewildered laugh.

Wyatt throws his hands in the air and proclaims, "Then, that's it! I pronounce you wed! *Now* you may—"

There isn't a second kiss. They are rushed by the waiting crowd, Lisi at the front, pulling them into embraces. Strangers kiss their cheeks and clap them on the back, the smell of alcohol on their clothes and laced among their encouraging words. Joy is refracted through the crowd like a prism. When Josie smiles sheepishly, they beam. When Lisi squeaks, "That's my cousin!" to a nearby stranger, a roar of unbridled rapture reverberates through the congregation for nearly a full minute.

They are herded against a plain wall where a man appears with a polaroid camera. Gabe and Josie shuffle into place on a line demarcated by faded masking tape.

"Stand like that . . . yes, perfect, that's exactly it," the man says. He pauses as they settle into position, getting a clear look at Josie. "It's a shame you've got a shiner for your wedding photographs."

"What?" Josie absently presses his fingers to his cheek, which aches at his touch. The attack at the motel feels like another lifetime. It makes Josie realize it's been just as long since he's looked into a mirror. He shrinks behind Gabe, abashed, combing his fingers through his hair.

"Do I look okay?" he asks, turning to Gabe.

"Of course you do," says Gabe.

"Big smiles!" the man behind the camera says. "With teeth!"

So Josie turns to the camera and smiles, with teeth.

Lisi pockets the picture for safekeeping as Gabe and Josie continue to politely battle back the well-intentioned crowd of wassailers.

"We're gonna take this across the street," says Wyatt, having wound his way back to them through the crowd.

"Thank you again, but we really should go," Gabe says.

"You don't want dinner?"

Lisi perks up. "You guys have food?"

Wyatt hinges back and bleats a loud laugh. "Do we have food?" he repeats incredulously. "Honey, we are in the center of extravagance and food is spoiling by the minute. We don't eat, we *feast*."

"We really can't stay long," says Josie, but his tongue has grown heavy in his mouth, salivating at the idea of a hot meal.

"So then don't stay long," says Wyatt. "We're just going across the highway, there."

They follow cautiously, herded by the general merriment, into an empty reception hall at the back of one of the lavish hotels along the strip, adorned at every turn with painted frescos and plaster cherubs mounted atop dry fountains and armless marble statues, all meant to evoke Italian palazzos. There are already groups there—some who seem to recognize the incoming crowd of revelers, others who barely look up from their own celebrations—all surrounding a long table piled high with food.

"Oh," Josie gulps, his usual wariness draining away as he catches a waft of grilled meat. "Pork chops."

They indulge in food and champagne—even Josie, who demurs for the reason of driving, but is cajoled into a glass as a wedding toast. There is a sense of wickedness, a childish feeling of getting away with something, that is spurred by the indulgence.

Lisi, in particular, had gotten extremely liberal with the refills of champagne. She tops off her glass, and then Gabe's, and coos, "I'm glad you got married. I really am."

"Thank you, chickadee," says Gabe, patting her hand, which is splayed wide on the tabletop.

She looks hard into Gabe's eyes from beneath her very furrowed brow. "I would never tell anyone that it wasn't real or anything," she swears, with her index finger held upright, a little too close to her face. The gesture slowly wilts, the effort of keeping the finger both straight and aloft proving a little too difficult. "Because it's real to us, and that's what matters."

Her face has gone pink, her dark eyes sparkling. The champagne glass seems too heavy in her other hand, wobbling dangerously close to spilling. "I can't believe I'm going to die single," she laments. "I mean, I don't think I'm all that special but as a person I think I'm—you know—*compelling*."

"You compel me," says Gabe, nodding back very seriously.

"You're teasing me!"

"No, no," Gabe insists, frowning in an overly dour, exaggerated way. "I would never."

Lisi laughs, but there is an inkling of hurt there. Josie discerns it with ease. Perhaps Gabe—handsome and easy as he is—is not familiar with that particular kind of loneliness and the intrinsic fear of an eternal lack of connection that comes with it. But Josie certainly recognizes it after agonizing decades of distancing himself from his own identity and desires.

"Lisi," Josie interrupts. "I think you are."

Lisi realizes she's been caught being earnest. She seems to spit the sentimentality out like a seed, dissolving into a stiff, reflexive laughter. "Oh my god, I'm *kidding*," she scoffs, and her hand dances in the air between them spasmodically. "Who cares."

Josie thinks it's understandable that she does care. But that topic has been quite resolutely shuttled, and it won't be brought up again.

Gabe beckons Wyatt over, who teeters over to their end of the table jovially, red-faced and inebriated.

"Wanna get married again?" he japes, gripping both of Josie's shoulders from behind and jostling him a little too enthusiastically. Josie grimaces but bites his tongue.

"We're actually hoping you can help us with something else," Gabe says, shrugging on his charms like a well-fitted jacket. Josie notes it instantly—the way he leans forward on his long forearms, his warm smile, the alluring mischief in his eyes. "Since you're the mayor around here, wouldn't you say?"

Wyatt titters. "Wouldn't say *that*," he says, but smiles a bit and protests no further.

"We're in a bit of a rut, here," Gabe explains. "We still need to get to California, but we're running low on gas. It's what brought us to Vegas in the first place."

"Tough situation," Wyatt says, nodding. "Tough indeed."

After a fair amount of nodding, and little else, Gabe presses, "So I'm hoping you might know a place to get some."

Wyatt whistles through his teeth, reeling back on his heels. "Like I said. Tough. Pretty bleak, even here." He gestures behind him at the teeming, inebriated crowd. "Lotta these people came to visit, ended up stranded." He shrugs. "Making the most of it though, ain't they?"

"What if we can't do that, though?" Lisi says, rising slowly out of her seat. "What if we can't die here?"

Gabe has his hand on her arm in an instant, urging her back, a technicolor smile on his face all the while. Josie admires that about him. Gabe can gauge a stranger's rhythms and humor in an instant and play right to them, if he wants. He knows exactly when to stand tall and assert himself or adopt a friendly, unassuming hunch.

"So true, so true," Gabe heralds grandly, suddenly also a preacher of the Vegas strip. "What a way to end it all."

Wyatt nods back.

"But we do need to get to California, is the thing. And we need gas to get there."

Wyatt considers this for a while, sucking on his bottom lip. "You could try and get to the real fancy parts of town," he suggests. "Summerlin North. Tule Springs. Might be some gas stations off the beaten path."

Lisi jots down the names of those places on her phone, nodding as she follows along.

"If there's not a gas station with anything left, there will be nice cars that got abandoned, I'm sure of that."

Lisi looks up from her phone. "Abandoned?"

"Sure. Second or third family cars that got left behind." Wyatt waggles his eyebrows and quips, "Rich people stuff."

"What does that—"

"Siphon whatever gas you need outta the tanks," Wyatt states plainly, like it should be obvious. "Or steal the whole car, if that's easier!"

Josie feels a genuine sense of elation. The idea would have never occurred to him.

They dismiss themselves summarily, afraid to get roped into any further debauchery, and peel off into the sunset. Without directions, it takes them a while to find any of the neighborhoods Wyatt had mentioned, largely choosing to follow a trail of nice grocery stores and fancy houses. It takes them up a winding canyon road to a sprawling stretch of abandoned houses on a dead-end street, each one larger and more ostentatious than the last.

Josie parks at the far end of a large cul-de-sac. Lisi is off like a shot, loping toward the house with the largest attached garage. She wrestles with the garage door comically, lying flat on the pavement to try and wedge something between the metal and the ground.

As Gabe goes to stop her, she snaps upright with a start. "Hold on," she says and darts around the side of the house. Josie and Gabe follow, watching her rise onto her toes, craning her long arm awkwardly over the wooden fence that cordons off the gigantic, manicured backyard. Gabe thinks she must be fumbling for a hidden latch. She stays there for a very long time, grunting with the effort, losing her balance over and over, and still can't seem to open it.

"I think it's just a fence, Lisi," Josie calls after her, beginning to feel a bit embarrassed for her efforts. But just as he says so, she erupts with a whooping sound of glee and darts toward them, holding a small gold key above her head triumphantly.

"There was a spare key nailed to the inside of the fence," she explains proudly, out of breath. "Our neighbors in Sacramento did that too."

Lisi unlocks the grand front door without incident. They hardly notice what's inside the home, searching only for the entrance to the covered garage. Lisi finds the door first and calls for Gabe and Josie as she pushes it open.

Two cars have been left behind in the garage, in near pristine condition.

"That's enough," Josie rasps, his throat constricted by shock. "That must be enough."

They stand there, merely studying the cars in silence, drinking in such long-awaited relief. They stagger back into the main foyer, a rising giddiness lapping at their heels.

In their satisfaction, they are finally able to absorb the home they've broken into. It is not just large, but labyrinthine, with a grand staircase that splits, leading to two separate second-floor landings. Even the palatial living room seems to have smaller, more specific living spaces delineated within it, with their own couches and televisions and coffee tables, adorned at every turn with crystal light fixtures and gigantic gold-framed mirrors. Towering windows overlook a sparkling backyard and pool, littered with loose plant matter in its disuse, but breathtakingly landscaped and appointed.

Unwilling to believe their luck, Josie goes to a low table and runs his finger over the surface. It comes up dusty. "No one's been here for a while."

"Who would leave a place like *this*?" Lisi squeaks.

"People with even bigger homes," Josie says, examining a fancy loveseat in the foyer. He has no sense of its purpose, too low and rigid for any real comfort and so thoroughly brocaded it can't be soft. "Or people with elaborate bunkers," he adds, craning his head up the grand, curving staircase.

Lisi gasps. "My god. Do you really think there are rich people in bunkers right now? Is, like, Matt Damon in a bunker?"

"Is that someone you know?" asks Josie, but before Lisi can splutter her flabbergasted response, Gabe scoffs loudly, his eyes rolling up to the bright, vaulted ceiling.

"Stupid, if they are," he says, spat with bitter distaste. "People who can't accept death."

Every room is somehow a surprise, as though each has been renovated in the *decor du jour* of a separate season. Gaudy, unfriendly in its excess, but overflowing with convenience. The pantry is not just stocked but overfilled. Lisi squeals, discovering an entire refrigerator dedicated just to alcohol. They talk in circles about what they should take with them on the road—perishables, clothing, electronics, wine?—knowing the remaining journey isn't long, but there will certainly be no opportunity to restock.

The ultra-modern living room features a towering mirror set in a stately marble-tile frame. They are all equally compelled by it, freezing in front of the daunting reflection.

"God," Lisi breathes. "We look like shit."

She isn't wrong. They have the quality of badly recalled caricatures of themselves, posture cricked from the long cramped hours in the car, unwashed hair hanging flat in their eyes. Josie's denim jacket is discolored from when the burglar had tackled him into the gravel parking lot. His face is unfamiliarly sunken—perhaps dehydrated, perhaps he'd lost weight—but his high, cherubic cheeks cast shadows over his dull, sallow skin. Gabe and Lisi look particularly unlike themselves in rumpled clothing that hangs unattractively on the frame of their angular bodies—Gabe looking thin in his plain white T-shirt, now stained and saggy, Lisi's cropped leather jacket shrunken and waxy and too tight in the shoulders. All three share a shiny vacancy in their eyes from a lack of truly good sleep. It is almost transfixing; they can't look away.

"We probably should stay the night," Gabe says, fussily combing his fingers through his limp hair.

"Of course," Lisi affirms quickly. "It's already late!"

"Can't hurt to sleep in a real bed for a night," says Gabe, and he leans down to press his lips against the top of Josie's head beside him. "Shower off," he continues lowly. "Right?"

Josie nods stiffly and clears his throat. "Better to leave well rested," he agrees. "Might be able to do the last stretch to Sacramento in one push tomorrow."

"Or whenever," says Lisi, failing to sound casual, "I don't have to get home *that* fast." At Gabe's raised eyebrow she protests, "It's your *honeymoon*, isn't it? You don't wanna try the pool?"

Gabe's hand lingers at the small of Josie's back; his answer is obvious. Josie is intensely aware that they are now the intruders, the plunderers, descended like vultures for some beer and fine bedding. But with so few remaining days, it has become increasingly difficult to care.

The primary bedroom upstairs is bedecked in cream and gold, with a plush, tufted headboard. It nearly gives Josie pause, the guilt of sleeping in a couple's abandoned bed palpable, but no more pressing than his very present desire to sleep on a large mattress next to Gabe.

"After you, sir," Gabe quips, ushering Josie inside. "I hope you'll find the accommodations to your liking."

Josie showers first, stunned at the color of the rivulets of water that spout off his shoulders and into the drain. The red dust in his hair must be from their day at the Grand Canyon. When the water finally runs clear, he gets out of the shower and scoops up his jeans and shirt from the vanity. It is only now, scrubbed clean and perfumed with a stranger's assorted soaps, that Josie realizes how badly his clothes smell.

He emerges from the bathroom in a borrowed plush bathrobe. It is comically overlarge on him; he has to walk carefully so as not to trip over the dragging hem.

Gabe reclines against the headboard, already in his boxers. His eyes scan Josie hungrily, from the top of his head down to his bare feet. Josie cannot help but squirm, feeling less like an eager honeymooner and more like a child who'd stolen their parents' clothing.

"My clothes don't smell very good," Josie explains, looking apologetically at the bundle in his hands. "I have spares in my bag, but it's downstairs."

"Don't," Gabe exhorts, long arm jutting out to point at Josie. He gesticulates toward Josie's robe. "Seriously. Don't . . . do . . . anything."

Gabe leaps up from the bed and toward the vacant bathroom. "Let me shower," he says. "I'll go fast. Jo, I'll be *so* mad if you put on clothes."

Josie alights at the edge of the bed, raising his palms in surrender.

Gabe fixes him with a final comically stern look, and then disappears into the bathroom in one giant, cartoonish side step, as if plucked from a silent film. It is heartening to see Gabe so untroubled, enjoying himself so thoroughly. It will be nice to *be* enjoyed, Josie's mind supplies. The anticipation fizzes in Josie's nose like champagne bubbles. Still, while Gabe is gone, he is mindful to kick his soiled clothes fully underneath the bed.

Josie learned a lot very quickly when he left his hometown. He escaped Ohio in the dead of night in Mister Ediger's car—it had long been promised to Josie, like many promises he suspected were told merely to keep him around—and drove the full eight hours to Manhattan in one itchy, adrenaline-fueled stretch. He sold the stolen car for the last six thousand dollars needed to pay for his housing and tuition, prayed forgiveness for the transgression, and began classes three days later. At first, everything shocked him: the constantly updating variety of music, the advanced technology of so many personal devices, how many people his age had everything paid for by their parents.

But the expected degree of personal grooming was a particular shock. Josie was flabbergasted by the cost of haircuts, which used to come free at his eldest sister's convenience. People seemed to own so many items of clothing; wearing a piece until it was threadbare was not a point of pride as it had been at home, but of unprofessionalism. The men Josie admired from afar seemed to exist in an unassailable echelon of urbanity, Josie like an archaic model of the same species. He was invisible to them, which had wounded his pride, but nonetheless allowed him to skate through life unbothered, without any prying questions into his past.

Gabe materializes a few minutes later, nude and still quite wet. "I hurried," he says simply, advancing on Josie. "I wanted to catch you."

"Catch me?" Josie means to question, but sound is sucked out of his lungs, Gabe's hand suddenly on Josie's chest, pressing him back against the mattress. It depresses plushly beneath their shared weight, not a sound out of the box spring. Gabe descends on him ravenously, kissing Josie deeply with one hand on the bed, the other hand fisting in the back of Josie's damp hair.

"Can you remember the last time we kissed like this?" Gabe asks, rising for air. Josie, for what it's worth, remains entirely breathless.

"Uh-uh," is all Josie can manage.

"Probably since before I was sick," says Gabe.

Josie's brow furrows. "That can't be true," he protests. He knows it very well might be true. Fear blurred their last three years together into an incomprehensible watercolor of heightened emotions.

"You have no idea how obsessed I am with you," Gabe mutters against Josie's temple. Josie can feel Gabe's warm exhale ghosting over the shell of his ear. "You really have no idea. When I first got sick, I used to try and imagine your next boyfriend just to train myself not to get blindingly jealous."

"Gabe," Josie gasps. "That's . . ." He wriggles out from under the pen of Gabe's arms, fixing Gabe with a chastising look.

Gabe merely looks up at him demurely, his head resting against Josie's stomach. "It's okay. The boyfriend you have after I die is really handsome," Gabe appeals, gently thumbing Josie's sour, downturned mouth. "And that makes me happy."

"There *is* no boyfriend."

"You have that friend at work that you always share lunch with," Gabe says, pushing himself upright to sit on his knees. "They're a teacher." He pauses for a moment, gaze flicking toward the ceiling as he searches for the name. "Robin."

"Robin is a woman. In her sixties."

Gabe does not have the decency to look properly abashed; he merely shrugs. "What if it was someone really rich? I could see you dating a doctor. You've always had a way of talking with doctors."

"I don't like this," Josie snaps, pulling his robe closed over his chest. "It's all made up. I don't like talking about made-up things."

Gabe's lips twitch, barely suppressing his amusement, nor his arousal at being so thoroughly scolded.

"And we might've had *years* together still," says Josie. "You don't know."

Gabe looks away. His silence feels spiny; less that he has nothing to say, so much as something he will not. But before Josie can find the words to prod him, Gabe has rubber-banded back into wolfishness.

"You're right," he croons, leaning in to cradle the back of Josie's head in one of his wide, warm palms. "What am I doing talking about handsome doctors on our wedding night? What if you decide to leave me?"

"I wouldn't," says Josie flatly.

"Everyone says divorce is monstrous, but I think we would have been amicable about it," Gabe muses, pinching Josie's chin between his thumb and forefinger. "Because of our incredible shared maturity."

Josie cracks, feeling the tug of a burgeoning smile. "You get the furniture and electronics," he counters. "I get the apartment."

"Why do you get the apartment?"

Josie catches his tongue between his front teeth and adopts as serious a tone as he can manage. "Because," he says very slowly. "I make all the money."

"This is madness," Gabe growls, slotting his knee between Josie's thighs. Josie gasps in happy surprise, turning to bury his face against his shoulder. Gabe seizes upon the exposed stretch of neck with his teeth, startling a cry out of Josie. "You're taking advantage of me, your poor wedded husband. I didn't sign a prenup and now I'm utterly ruined."

"Oh god, Gabe," Josie gasps, "Are we doing this? This isn't our bed."

"It's just a hotel," Gabe murmurs into his ear. "It's our honeymoon."

TWELVE DAYS

Josie pries himself out of a light and comfortable doze, ravenous for cold water. He disentangles himself from beneath Gabe's heavy arm and pads downstairs in the dark, proceeding slowly through the unfamiliar layout of the large house. An illuminated clock on the microwave in the kitchen shows that it's past midnight, but doesn't provide quite enough light for Josie to find the fancy recessed light switches. The only lights that are on are the ones built into the lawn by the pool. Josie peers out and finds Lisi sitting in one of the pool chairs, a beer in one hand, her phone in the other. She is wearing an over-large set of flannel pajamas that look as if they were pilfered from a teenage boy's bedroom. There is something melancholic about the silhouette: Lisi alone in a warm wash of light, except for her face—features sharp, chiseled, cold—illuminated by the blue light of the phone screen, presiding over a dark and empty domain from her throne.

He slides the glass door open.

Lisi snaps toward the sound as Josie steps out into the yard. Her expression blooms with panic. Josie's stomach plummets, horrified to have frightened her so badly. Long hair still damp from her own shower, bare-faced and without the armor of her usual carefully-cultivated clothing, she looks alarmingly childlike.

Before Josie can manage the first syllable of an apology, Lisi has expertly shaken it off, tucking both the phone and bottle between her knees so that she can clap enthusiastically in his direction.

She reaches into a cooler at her feet and extends a cold beer his way. "Cheers," she says, and turns the bottle in her wrist, as if modeling it. "Really spectacular work. You deserve it."

The beer, glass-bottled, beaded with crisp condensation, looks more appealing than anything Josie can ever recall wanting. He reaches for it, then suddenly pauses and lowers his hand.

"What work?" he asks.

Lisi only quirks a wry, knowing eyebrow.

"No," Josie says, in the same tone someone might chastise a wayward dog. "You didn't hear . . ."

Lisi grins, her hand posed cherubically beneath her chin.

"Lisi!"

"You two *drove* me out here, I wasn't *trying* to hear anything!" she protests. At Josie's rankled expression she adds, "But you didn't make it easy."

"You didn't hear," Josie repeats, now more like a command.

"I could share with you some of the greatest hits."

"Don't," Josie warns her, snatching the proffered beer from her hand. "*Don't.*"

He sinks into the lawn chair beside her, cracks off the cap on the metal arm, and downs most of the bottle in one long, grateful gulp. "Is there service here?" he asks Lisi, who is sliding her cell phone back into the pocket of her pajama pants.

"Oh," says Lisi with a measure of surprise, as if she'd been caught doing something untoward. "No. Everything is still down. I was just checking."

She chews her bottom lip in the stilted silence that follows. Josie never quite understood Lisi's obsession with regaining the use of her cell phone. At first, he'd assumed it had to do with how far they were from Sacramento, and the need to inform her parents of their progress. But now, only a day or two's drive away from home, her palpable upset seems misplaced. Nonetheless, merely the mention of her cell phone has soured her mood, and Josie is surprised to find himself feeling guilty.

"If only you were more interested in finding a working phone than on what we were doing inside . . ." he chides. Josie doesn't like to be goaded, but Lisi enjoys winding him up, so he decides to be merciful and allow her the distraction.

"I'll forgive you, Josie," she says, taking his bait without hesitation. "It's traditional to fuck on your wedding night."

"Don't say that," Josie admonishes.

"What? Fuck?"

"Yes."

"Oh, I forgot you don't curse."

"Yes, I do!" Josie answers petulantly. "Just not . . ." He pauses and searches for the word, distracted by Lisi's rapt, mischievous expression and the oncoming swoon of inebriation. ". . . *unnecessarily*," he concludes.

"Would you say fuck?"

"I guess," Josie shrugs. "I know I've said it before."

"Ooh, what about cunt?" she asks, extending her leg so that her foot pokes into Josie's thigh. "Would you say that?"

"Absolutely not, that's the worst word. It's so sexist."

"Actually, the fact that you *think* it's the worst word is what's sexist."

"You know, Lisi," Josie says, the round mouth of his beer bottle pressed against his lower lip, "you don't have to say things out loud if you know they're stupid."

Lisi throws her head back and cackles. "Josie!" she gasps between peals of laughter. "That was such a bitchy thing to say!"

Josie sinks down lower into the lawn chair as if willing it to swallow him, face purpling with embarrassment but still grinning behind his beer bottle.

"You little bitch," Lisi hoots.

Josie cannot hide his delight. He hinges at the waist, slumped over himself, cheek pressed into his kneecap. "Ouch," he wheezes, convulsing with laughter. "Oh, I'm drunk."

Lisi hums, rolling the sound around in her mouth as if it were a hard candy.

"What," says Josie, looking at her askance from atop his knees.

"Maybe I'm drunk," she lilts, teasing and fond, "but right now I see it."

Josie rights himself with some effort. He touches his cheeks, ruddy and warmed both from the alcohol and the blood that has rushed to his head. "What?"

"I feel like I'm seeing you how Gabe sees you," she says, lifting her right hand into the shape of an L and squinting past it, as if framing Josie in a camera. "Or maybe it's just your boxers . . ."

"Oh, hush," Josie snaps.

The night is dark, and some sort of late summer bug hums in the trees. Lisi's laugh rings out over the treetops, clear and buoyant as music. Josie happily succumbs to his inebriation, to the unexpected ease of sitting beside Lisi in the quiet, watching how she idly swings her ankle in a figure-eight pattern exactly the same way Gabe does.

Gabe holds court in his usual way once the show comes down, cast and audience alike filtered into the main vestibule. It is an unfamiliar venue. Josie does not know the ins and outs, the places Gabe likes to post up to receive his fans, the names of the friendly and overworked bartenders who automatically open Gabe's tab. Josie aimlessly circles the lobby a few times until he finds Gabe perched against a cocktail table, already in his street clothing with his duffle bag slung over his shoulder. Gabe casts out his arm as if plucking Josie out of a riptide, downs the last of the frosty bottle of water in his other hand, and tugs Josie in for a brief and icy kiss.

"Oops, sorry," Gabe says, thumbing a stray bead of water off the underside of Josie's chin. "Glad you found me."

"Sorry?" Josie questions, with his hand to his ear. "I can't hear you." He is jostled by the overlarge backpack of a passing performer angling toward his own gaggle of friends. Josie had never seen such a large cast of dancers in a show before, and the theater can barely house both the performers and their awaiting audience.

Gabe posts his forearms up onto Josie's shoulders, leaning forward over him. He ducks his head so that his mouth is against Josie's ear.

"I'm ravenous," says Gabe lowly, in lieu of a greeting.

"Should we find some place around here? We can invite your friends." Josie inquires, tilting his head back to meet Gabe's eyes. The strange posture briefly throws him off balance, but Gabe instinctively counters, leaning just enough weight down into Josie's shoulders to steady him.

"Nah, I wanna go home," he answers. "Cab's on me."

Gabe flags one down quickly and pats Josie's hip to encourage him inside first.

"The show, um," Josie says once they've settled into their seats and are heading uptown. "I thought it was interesting."

"Interesting?"

"I can tell it took a lot of rehearsal."

Gabe laughs. "That's textbook for: *I hated it, and I don't have anything else to say.*"

Josie squawks a small noise of indignation, jabbing his index finger toward Gabe in the adjacent seat. "That is not what I meant," he protests. "I meant there were a lot of dancers on stage."

Gabe's smirk is utterly feline, the pleased hunter with the canary. "But did you *like* it?"

Josie opens his mouth, and then quickly closes it.

"Please, tell me," Gabe goads laughingly. He snatches Josie's hand and squeezes it hard between both of his own. "Come on."

"I think," Josie hedges, "maybe I just prefer your choreography."

Gabe's mouth pinches tight around a barely suppressed huff of laughter. "And why's that?"

Josie can only shrug.

"All of the dancers dressed similarly, moving similarly . . . you're meant to experience us as like, one body." Gabe demonstrates this as well, swinging his neck from side to side, his hands winding deftly around each other.

"Okay," answers Josie, unsure of what else to say. He had not gleaned such a thing out of the tedium of the performance, in which Gabe largely danced in the back.

This answer, however, spears Gabe with a bolt of uproarious laughter. Josie must not hide his indignity well, as Gabe immediately pushes himself into Josie's seat, grabbing Josie's knee almost a little too hard. "No, sorry, sorry," Gabe wheezes, trying and failing to right his distinctly delighted expression. His voice still bounces on the exhalations of a giggle. "I'm sorry. I'm not laughing at you. I honestly love when you don't love it."

"I just want to watch *you*," Josie protests, feeling the prickly warmth of a blush creeping up his neck. "Is that such a crime?"

"I *love* it when you watch me," Gabe answers, flipping the hard L in *love* over his teeth luxuriously. Josie's eyes feel stuck on Gabe's slightly wet lower lip. Gabe smells like sweat and powder and wet stone. Josie claws his cotton scarf away from his very flushed neck just as Gabe seizes upon the bare stretch of skin with his teeth.

Josie's eyes catch those of the cab driver, watching them in the rearview mirror. He swats at Gabe's shoulder until Gabe detaches himself and slides back into his own seat.

"Wanna come to a Halloween party next weekend?" Gabe asks, infuriatingly nonchalant, scratching at the corner of his mouth with his thumbnail. "Costumes not required. The rooftop's nice too."

"Whose party?"

"Did you meet Marc Fontaine? Little guy. Red hair."

"I'm not sure."

"Director I know from Jacob's Pillow; he was briefly working with Lisi and her theater troupe," Gabe continues at his elevated pace, his long hands weaving about in the space between them as if conjuring the images out of thin air. "Oh! And Lisi will be there."

"Mm," says Josie. He catches Gabe looking askance, tracking Josie in his periphery.

There wasn't anything wrong with Lisi, of course. She was young and funny and ravenous for a good time. When it was the three of them together, Lisi brought out a rebellious quality in Gabe, a Gabe who sought out trouble and faced it, gleefully, head-on; swindling bouncers into allowing them into private events, sneaking off elevators at floors marked only for staff. There was nothing wrong with that Gabe. He was even—Josie had to admit—sort of excruciatingly, insouciantly sexy, and not at all like a person Josie imagined he'd ever be associated with. But Josie also felt he was the fourth invited guest: the Gabe that Josie could never meet alone.

Gabe turns to Josie. "I'd really like for you and Lisi to get to know each other better. I think you have a lot in common."

Josie feels the surprise register on his face before he is able to wrest his expression back to neutrality. It is too late; Gabe seizes on the moment.

"What's that face for?" he asks, reaching between them and prodding Josie's shoulder, once, with great theatricality.

"I," Josie begins, before realizing he doesn't have the words for what he wants to say—which lands somewhere between *If this is a joke, I don't like it* and *But you and Lisi are the ones who are alike*. But he must say something, so Josie manages, "What do we have in common?"

Gabe smiles, his dark eyes briefly ringed in neon blue as the cab passes beneath an illuminated sign. "That I love you," he answers with a very satisfied finality.

"I'll check my schedule," says Josie, which is enough to resolve the conversation for the time being.

"Fine," Gabe chirps, and then lowers his voice conspiratorially, "but go back. Tell me what else you hated about the show."

A week or so after Halloween, on a crisp and gorgeous November day, Gabe leaves for a routine doctor's appointment and doesn't return for six hours. When he finally arrives home, he shoots through the door, hot with indignation, into Josie's fretful domain. *It can't be true.*

They obviously want the insurance money. It's just headaches. Everyone gets headaches. I'm thirty years old, there's nothing wrong with my brain.

And later, when the flame has burned itself out and a terrible sadness has settled in, Gabe presses his cell phone into Josie's palm. "You have to tell Lisi," he rasps. "I can't. I won't be able to."

And Josie obeys.

SEVEN DAYS

A day turns into two, slips into three, then five; long, languid days eating and talking and reading books in the indulgent, generator-run air conditioning. Gabe and Josie are rarely out of bed, so Lisi borrows an ill-fitting turquoise bathing suit from one of the bedrooms and is rarely out of the pool.

It blissfully recalls the earliest days of their relationship, untroubled by sickness and loans and the daily injustices that simmer over the heat of so much anger with no clear place to express it.

Gabe is insistent and tender with Josie, then sleeps long, long hours, sometimes through large parts of the day. He rejects any of Josie or Lisi's concern, blaming it on his unusually relaxed state. Instead, he deflects by encouraging Josie to go swimming with Lisi, or by pointedly musing on Josie's *stamina*, until Josie blushes too much to continue his line of questioning.

Lisi has learned to leave them their space. It's no chore; with Gabe and Josie sequestered to the bedroom, the rest of the mansion has become her private domicile. The remaining days until Impact dwindle into the single digits. She sprawls out on her stomach on the white shag carpet in the living room, sampling from four bags of different chips for lunch. She wrestles the old portable DVD player in the den into playing the copy *of You've Got Mail* left inside it and watches it three times in a day, until it is nearly committed to memory, and then performs one of the key monologues for the audience of herself, into the mirror. The pool is spacious and sun-warmed. The Wi-Fi doesn't work, despite her many attempts. The old landlines she's found in the home office don't work either. She cracks open an expensive, glass-bottled water while swimming. She eats the cereal dry. She checks her cell phone for signal. She looks for more DVDs. She checks the Wi-Fi. She returns to the pool.

Once the hysteria hits her, it is too massive and too impossible to untangle reasonably. It had been encroaching, like fire lapping her ankles, but the luxurious change of pace from the road had given her just enough fuel to outrun it for a time.

It spears her, hard, on her morning swim, when she suddenly realizes she hasn't heard the sound of birds in days.

Dripping wet, towel forgotten by the deck chairs, she stumbles dizzily back into the house. The cold, air-conditioned air meets her like a brick wall. It is enough to jolt her out of the hot grip of panic and into the icy stillness of grief. The house is quiet. It is always quiet, with Gabe and Josie cloistered away. And so she sinks to her knees on the carpet, buries her face in her hands, and wails.

"Lisi?"

Lisi snaps to attention, finding a mussed-looking Josie framed in the great arch of the living room entryway.

"What happened?" he presses, just as she dissolves into a new, uncontrollable barrage of tears.

"Go back upstairs, Josie, I'm fine," she warbles. She'd meant to sound stern but has enough awareness to hear how pathetic she sounds.

She stares at his bare feet, which do not move.

"I'm not sure I should," he says.

"Where're the birds?"

There's another long pause before Josie manages a hollow, "Sorry?"

"Please go upstairs," Lisi restates pleadingly. "I just need a minute."

"I don't want to. I'm worried—"

"I haven't had service since New York," she explodes, the relentless unhappiness propelling her to her feet. "I thought maybe these people'd have Wi-Fi or something, but I guess that's gone, just like the power." Her hands fist in her wet hair, which leaves dark droplets on the cream-colored carpet in her wake as she paces. "And my phone is running out of battery constantly, because all it's doing is searching for a signal, so then I think, *Just turn it off! Throw it in the car! Who cares?*"

Lisi gulps for breath, the cold, thin air like a knife in her throat.

"But what if that's the one time messages come through?" she continues, jabbing a finger in the air emphatically. She inhales to speak, but her voice cracks, rib cage caving in like a kicked soda can. "What if it's the one time I can say goodbye?"

Josie is stiff and unblinking, the posture of an animal weighing when to scurry away, hoping to blend into the background. It makes Lisi feel very guilty and very small.

"Never mind," she says, scrubbing her hands over her face. Her cheeks feel swollen and feverish against her numb fingertips.

"But, Lisi," Josie counters, in a small voice reedy with discomfort, "we'll get you home soon. I transferred out the gas today and everything."

"It's not that," she protests, digging the heels of her hands into her eyes. The world had seemed so expansive as they were traveling, their destination impossibly far. Now, in their moment of rest, the universe extended only as far as the backyard, with Gabe and Josie the only company in all of the world. "I'm stupid, you don't have to tell me that." She laughs bitterly, running the back of her wrist across her mouth. "I just sort of assumed"—she hiccups sharply—"that I'd say goodbye to my friends."

The weeping roils over anew. She is embarrassed to be caught breaking down, but equally embarrassed to realize that she desperately wants Josie's comfort. Somewhere along their journey, the tender fastidiousness with which he treated Gabe had tipped from sweet to enviable.

She tries to push the hair out of her eyes, and her fingers become tangled at the crown of her head. "And my fucking hair is a wreck!" she shouts and stomps, completely given over to the unruly, childish chaos of her jumbled emotions.

"You aren't stupid," Josie says. He takes a long moment to consider, and then exhales, shaking his head. "I can't imagine how you feel. I know you had a lot of friends."

Lisi stares at him, searching for an angle of impatience or mockery. He'd always seemed dismissive of her large social circle and her carousel of new hobbies and interests and acquaintances, but she finds only his usual unadorned sincerity.

"It's okay, Josie," she says.

"It isn't, though," Josie insists. "Nothing is okay."

There's a sense of practicality to his statement, a keen awareness that is neither angry nor defeated. It's the same implacable pragmatism Lisi chafed at on the road, but she sees real comfort in it now.

"I think it'll be good for you to see your parents," he says, and Lisi nods stiffly. He begins to close the distance between them in small, even paces. "I think you might feel some . . ." Josie trails off, evaluating his words. Lisi can't help but wonder if it's a habit of his own or one absorbed from so much time with Gabe. She'd always admired Gabe's unwillingness to mince words, his thoughtful and measured consideration, when Lisi couldn't help but dart into everything, hackles already raised.

"Closure?" Lisi posits meekly.

Josie smiles. "Yes," he says. "That's exactly it."

She nods, feeling a small quaver of pride.

"We'll leave tomorrow. You'll be with them soon."

Slowly, Josie's hand, which had been hanging loosely at his side, lifts. It hangs momentarily in the space between them—pale and limp as a handkerchief—before settling over the cleft of Lisi's shoulder. She is icy from standing wet in the air-conditioned draft. He stands almost eerily still, as if bracing himself for Lisi to flinch away, but when she doesn't, he cups his other hand around her upper arm and gently rubs warmth back into her skin. His hands are cool and calloused. Lisi wonders how a person develops hands like that; it's certainly not from teaching children their consonants at a posh elementary school in Manhattan.

"You're going to get sick," he tuts, solicitous and fussy as ever.

Lisi shrugs. "Sorry you caught me, like, very much losing my shit."

Josie lifts his eyes and pins her with a knowing look. "With everything we've been through, it's probably good for us." His candor catches her by surprise, and she guffaws. He claps her arm bracingly before he steps back, looking irrepressibly pleased with himself for her reaction. "Not to mention, you saved my life."

That realization strikes Lisi like a dart between the eyes. "Shit!" she gulps. "Remember *that?*" Inadvertently, she goes to clutch the hair behind her ear, but her fingers catch in the unruly tangle. She curses under her breath. "I showered this morning and didn't brush my hair out, and then swam, and now—"

"Sit there," Josie directs, pointing to the low-backed loveseat in the corner.

Lisi manages a small, clipped noise of surprise, but Josie only waves her toward it with his usual frankness.

She settles on it, legs crossed, and Josie passes behind her. She cranes over her shoulder to watch him, unable to give voice to any of the myriad questions she could ask. He directs her gaze forward with a jut of his chin. She looks toward the empty pool, glistening in the late-afternoon sun, hearing nothing but Josie's even breathing behind her. He begins combing through her tangled hair with his fingers, piecing out sections, and winding them into a thick, even braid.

It is soothing. Hypnotic, even. And so easily, plainly compassionate that Lisi aches with relief. "You're fast," is all she can manage to say.

"Just practiced," says Josie. He swallows. "I have four sisters."

"Really?" she says, angling over her shoulder as much as she can without disrupting him. "I didn't know."

"Two older, two younger."

"Where are they?"

"I don't know," Josie answers honestly, the same way he always has when asked about his family.

"Well, I hope they're safe right now," Lisi adds, so guilelessly that Josie can only agree that he hopes so as well.

Gabe watches as Josie shoulders the bedroom door open in tentative touches; first there is a crack of light from the hallway, followed by just the dome of his blond head, until finally Josie appears in full, framed in the doorway. He seems genuinely staggered to find Gabe nude and lazing but, most importantly, awake.

"Hello," Gabe invites, with a waggle of his ankle.

"Gabe," says Josie, and then nothing else.

Gabe appraises Josie's stiff posture with suspicion. "Your shirt is wet," he says.

Josie looks down at his white T-shirt, spotted with water, and tuts at it admonishingly as though it could cough up an apology. "I was just helping Lisi with something," he answers patly. He says nothing more.

"Wanna come in?" Gabe invites.

"You're busy," says Josie with an unconvincing gesture toward the book in Gabe's hand. It is some pulpy paperback mystery with an ambiguous clock on the cover that Gabe had plucked off the bedside table and could not even recall the title of.

Gabe pointedly tosses it aside, then raises his empty palms like a magician.

"Can I talk to you about something?" says Josie. His voice is faltering and out of tune, like a woodwind instrument played incorrectly.

Gabe raises an eyebrow and is met with further silence. "Uh-oh. This seems serious."

"No, no," Josie assuages, and then, with a barely concealed wince, corrects himself. "Well, it is serious. But not because of anything you've done."

"Is it Lisi?"

"It isn't Lisi."

"Well then, uh-oh," Gabe repeats.

"It isn't anything you can do anything about," Josie adds, which only sets Gabe's spine even straighter.

Gabe leans over the side of the bed and snatches up his discarded shirt, which he slides into quickly. "You're scaring me," he says, and as Josie comes to sit beside him on the bed, he catches one of Josie's hands and pulls it into his own. "You're shaking, Jo—"

"Please don't be scared," Josie appeals quickly, leaning in to quiet Gabe with a kiss. He pleads against his mouth, "Please don't be scared, please."

Gabe cups Josie's cheek in his palm. His skin is both flushed and clammy.

"I always intended to tell you this," says Josie, "even if the world wasn't ending. Tonight just seemed like a good time."

"Okay," Gabe says, trying to sieve as much emotion out of his voice as he can. "Tell me."

"When we met, I told you I'd never kissed a man before," Josie says.

"Yes," Gabe affirms. "I remember that."

"That is true," says Josie. "I hadn't, until I met you." Josie sucks in a short breath. He pinches the inside of his wrist as he sweeps together the fragments of his next thoughts. "Because of that, you assumed that I had also never had sex with a man before. That is not true. But I never corrected you."

Gabe is immediately buffeted by a strong sense of relief. "Oh, baby," Gabe breathes, and tries to fight the indelicate smile that he feels tugging at the corners of his mouth. "Were you afraid I'd be mad if you told me?"

"No," Josie says. "I was afraid to tell you what it was like."

The severity of that statement winds the both of them, and it takes long moments for Josie to continue.

"What I mean is, it was not consensual. And it was not random. It was habitual, over years."

Gabe can only nod and is relieved that Josie seems to know what to say next, as he does not.

"I had a neighbor who was an older man. His arm was crushed by some farm machinery, and he won a lot of money from a lawsuit, but he needed help around his house. He would pay me to run his errands. Clean house. Cook dinner. I did do exactly that, for years. I don't know why it changed. But once he started, it became a, a, a very regular practice."

Gabe studies Josie's face—his flaring nostrils and quavering lower lip. But Josie only stares at the quilt.

"I was paid well. It relieved a burden on my family, with enough that I could save for myself." He then snorts a strange little half-laugh, one that catches in his throat and pitches his voice high. "I'd been told to stop asking about college. Now I wouldn't have to ask."

"You never told your family," Gabe posits, piecing together Josie's willful estrangement.

"No, I did," Josie corrects. "Twice."

"*Twice?*"

"I don't know," says Josie, his face reddening. "It seemed like the first time I said anything, they just"—he presses his fingers hard into his eyes—"forgot," he concludes.

"And the second time?"

"They tried to have me medicated," Josie answers.

"Why?"

"I don't know," says Josie flatly. "I don't know. It was their only response. I don't know if they still don't believe me."

Gabe says nothing.

"I did what I needed to do, until I had saved enough money. I came straight to New York. I worked, and I got my degrees, and that was it, there was no one else until . . ."

Me, thinks Gabe, recalling Josie's breathlessness at their first kiss, and the way he tremored from something more than the cold. Their relationship had unfolded quickly from there. Gabe had asked him to move in within the year. Everything was so simple with Josie, so easy; even the way that they both fell mutually evasive and laconic on the topic of their own families felt to Gabe like proof of their natural, destined compatibility. Gabe cannot help but find his mind wandering back to those early days, trying to follow the threads of what he might have done or said to earn Josie's trust. Or worse, to have betrayed it, without even knowing.

"You feel sick," Josie notes. "I can tell."

"No," says Gabe, deliberately quick to answer. "No. I'm only . . ." Josie seems both expectant and deeply, unshakably fearful of his next words, so Gabe takes time to consider them. "Josie, I'm stunned," is where Gabe arrives.

"I am aware that I lied to you, and for years."

"Jo," Gabe says firmly. "You didn't lie."

But Josie is caught up in his own momentum, warbling, "It was impossible not to. You were so sweet with me. Sweet and slow. No one had ever . . . it felt like starting over. Do you know what I mean? Do you?"

Gabe nods. He supposes he does know what Josie means, but to Gabe it seems much more important to merely affirm him, to let him empty himself of everything he'd withheld from Gabe for years.

"To have the chance to do it the right way? I mean, the way everyone else gets to? I was . . . was . . ." Josie's eyes roll back, trying to disguise his tears. "Gabe, I couldn't think about anything else when you were with me. Everything felt new."

"That's good," says Gabe, surprised by the thinness of his own voice, and unsurprised by his own tears that follow. "I'm glad I gave you something."

Josie sucks in a wet breath and exhales a skittering little laugh like the sound of a pebble kicked over pavement. "Gabe, you have no idea how much you gave me."

Gabe brushes a tear off the high apple of Josie's cheek and lets his hand linger there, dragging his fingernails lightly over the shell of his ear. "I don't know what to say," Gabe admits. Josie nods his understanding. Gabe knows any sort of platitudes, any stock prevaricating, would frighten Josie off of opening up any further. Nothing sickened Josie more than thin, protracted politeness.

"That's fine," Josie replies. "I don't want to talk about this anymore. My head hurts."

"Can I get you something? Water?" Gabe asks.

Josie has gone very quiet. Gabe studies him as he retreats inward, as Josie often does when overwhelmed. He thumbs Josie's light eyelashes.

"Baby," Gabe entreats, reaching for his attention. "I'm right here. Can I get you something?"

"Can we lie down?" Josie asks.

Gabe slides back against the pillows and guides Josie next to him, easing Josie's head onto his chest. Gabe concentrates hard, keeping his breathing even, synchronizing his inhalations with Josie's.

"Gabe?"

"Mm?"

"Were you in love with anyone else? Before me?"

Gabe considers the question. "No, I don't think I was," he answers truthfully. "I might have believed I was at the time. But it wasn't love."

"What made me special?" Josie asks, sounding abashed and needful in a way Josie rarely is. Josie is the admirer, the ever-present audience, diffident and uncomfortable in the heat of the spotlight.

"I don't know," Gabe says. "But you instantly were. I spotted you standing by the door in Dixon Place, and you were already special."

"You were beautiful," Josie exhales. Gabe feels a new wetness seeping through his shirt where Josie lies buried against him.

"You had matching gloves and hat," Gabe recollects. "I thought it was so funny."

"You didn't have a coat at all. Not a winter one."

"Irresponsible," says Gabe, a smile warming the sound of his voice. "That's me." He cups the back of Josie's neck, his thumb brushing up and down the small protrusions of his spine. "I never meant to say I was unlucky," he says, pressing his lips to the dome of Josie's head. "I'm sorry for all the times I did, and that I believed it."

Gabe feels Josie's hand curl tightly around his bicep. Gabe is grateful to be sturdy for him in this moment, to be an approximation of the warm, hale body Josie first thought was so beautiful. He speaks into the softness of Josie's hair, "I don't resent a life I spent any part of with you."

Gabe and Josie lie together in silence, cleaving to each other tightly as they parse through their fractured thoughts. Gabe was not aware that unhappiness and gratefulness could be intersecting emotions; the extremes of both felt in such force leave him queasy with motion sickness.

Gabe awakens with a start. "Baby?" he croaks at length. "Shit. Sorry." His words are slurred and heavy. He'd descended into a deep, inky sleep—the kind of exhaustion that overtakes in an instant—but has no sense of how long he's been unconscious. He swallows a pang of guilt and squeezes Josie around his soft shoulders. Josie was an unfaltering sentinel in his turns as Gabe's nurse and guard dog. Gabe is mortified to find himself so instantly, obviously lacking.

"I don't know when I got so tired," he mumbles past a slack and leaden jaw.

"Sleep," Josie whispers. "It's okay."

"Are you sure? We can talk."

Josie pats Gabe's chest reassuringly. Gabe is asleep again in an instant.

The next morning, as they are packing to leave, Gabe drops a plate in the kitchen.

"It's fine," he says before Josie can rush to clean it. "I've got it, I've got it."

It takes a very long time for Gabe to stoop to his knees. His head sways heavily on his neck.

"Gabe?"

"I feel fine," Gabe snaps. "Just a headache."

"I'll get you some water," Josie says, and scurries out of the room. When he returns, Gabe is still perched uneasily on his knees. The plate remains in shards on the floor.

"Hon," Josie starts, unable to disguise the warble in his voice. "I brought something for the migraines."

Gabe says nothing. He knows what Josie is working up the fortitude to say next.

"Did you put the anti-seizure medication somewhere else?"

"I ran out in Oklahoma," Gabe answers tersely. He doesn't have the energy to delay the inevitable argument. He's suddenly very, very tired. "Can you take me to the couch?"

TWO YEARS, FIVE MONTHS, AND TWENTY-TWO DAYS

Gabe knows something isn't right the moment he walks on stage. His breathing is too shallow. He can't find the plumb-line of his center of balance, and all his turns and spins leave him feeling dizzy and underwater. His fingers tremble in moments of extension.

And when Gabe catches Josie's face in the darkened audience, perched anxiously at the edge of his seat, his round eyes wet, fixed, and unblinking, Gabe instantly knows. Knows that Josie sees it too.

The realization distracts him. Gabe's knees buckle under his weight. He catches himself adeptly, rolling his unsure footing into a purposeful-looking catch step.

"We have reached the end of our show," Gabe announces, his voice like gravel. He turns a quaking palm out toward the audience. Toward Josie, whose knuckles are crushed against his lips. "Goodnight. See you when I see you."

Josie is Gabe's most faithful audience; an attentive, thoughtful second party, happy to spend long hours in a theater seat or sitting on the floor of a rehearsal studio, watching Gabe run through the same pass of choreography for an hour. Josie cannot articulate the artistry, or name the steps, or delineate why it is that the stamp and not the drag of a foot is more palpably felt by the audience, but his tastes are attuned, and he is honest, and can always sense when Gabe has arrived at what works. There is an energetic settling—the intersection of intention and execution.

After the show, Josie is waiting for Gabe in the lobby, near the door, in the same place where they first met. He beckons Gabe into a one-armed hug that Gabe doesn't quite return.

"Congratulations," Josie greets him, as he always does. Gabe doesn't look at him. His eyes rake over the groups of mingling strangers with a barely concealed vitriol, his expression shielded by the low brim of his black baseball cap.

"You saw," Gabe says tersely.

"What?"

"That it wasn't good," Gabe clarifies. "You know that."

Josie does know. Josie has invested long and loving hours into knowing everything about Gabe's dancing, and Gabe is grasping for his frank and familiar honesty like a lifeboat in a storm.

But instead, Josie bobs his shoulders in a meek shrug. "You may have done better shows," he counters diplomatically. "But I'm sure no one else noticed."

Gabe scans the crowd in agitated silence, fiddling with his collar. He grumbles, "If they can accept that this is me at my best, I should kill myself now."

"Gabe," Josie prevaricates wanly, largely to the back of Gabe's denim jacket as he sullenly stomps away.

Gabe beelines to the exit as quickly as he can, trying his best to stay unnoticed and out of the aim of any pat or undeserved praise. He pushes out onto the street, Josie at his heels and breathless from the pursuit.

"Gabe, Gabe," Josie calls out, now free of the buzz of lobby chatter and the press of strange bodies. "Gabe, where are you going?"

Gabe says nothing, stalking up and down a short stretch of the city block, rapidly vacillating between fury and bald-faced heartbreak.

"Try and think about the week you've had," Josie appeals earnestly. "You've never tried to dance after—you know—a cycle like that."

Gabe's usual instinct is to reject speaking about his treatment so vaguely when they both fully understand Josie's polite intimation. His oncologist had pressed for a somewhat more aggressive course of action after a disappointing first five months of on-and-off chemotherapy. Gabe had spent the last two weeks in the clinic three consecutive days at a time—long, arduous stretches in a chair with an IV in his arm. Mondays included chelation treatment before chemotherapy, leaving him out of commission for five or six hours. Josie always arrived harried and apologetic after dismissal at school, flashing his visitor badge in an almost comically manic way at anyone who passed, scanning for Gabe.

Josie's point was fair, as were all things with Josie. Things had escalated. Adjustment was necessary.

Change had always been difficult, but it had been incremental, assailable, and reasoned away. Gabe couldn't count the amount of well-intentioned nurses and lab technicians who countered him with a flimsy, "How lucky that you're so young and healthy." Now it seems seismic. Planetary. Gabe swallows back panic thickly.

"Let's just get home," he says curtly. "I want to take a shower."

Gabe's legs bow again as he turns, steadying himself against the railing of a nearby brownstone. Josie stays close in his wake, his hand hovering just behind the concave of Gabe's lower back.

"Let me hail a cab," Josie appeals. Gabe opens his mouth to protest but is too winded to manage much more than a displeased wheeze. "Please, it's fine," Josie says. "I have the money."

Gabe hates when Josie says things like that, so sweetly and so dismissively. It only succeeds in making Gabe feel smaller and more piteous. But his exhaustion has tipped into a very sharp and very present nausea, so he can only nod as Josie shuffles him into a cab.

The cab driver glances contemptuously at the two of them collapsed against each other in the back seat.

"He's not drunk, right?" the driver asks, just a pair of eyes in a rearview mirror.

"Just tired," Josie snaps defensively. "So we'd appreciate getting home quickly."

Josie all but carries Gabe up the three flights of stairs to their apartment. Gabe can hardly lift his feet to assist. Partly, it's because any physical effort spears him with a cold, clammy nausea. But also, there is a part of him that wants to be unresponsive, obstinate, not like the regular, everyday Gabe, because he feels so completely alien to himself. With immense difficulty, Josie wrangles him bodily through the front door. Gabe stumbles to the living room and collapses in a boneless heap on the floor.

There is an odd sense about such heightened hysteria. Gabe feels outside his own body, looking down at the comically overdramatic image of himself sprawled on the floor with the crook of his elbow flung over his eyes. *That isn't what sadness looks like*, he thinks. *That's only in movies*. But it is not a movie, and it is very much the despondency he feels.

Josie kneels at Gabe's hip, hovering over him apprehensively. He rests his fingers lightly against Gabe's trembling chin. "I think a shower would do us good."

Gabe says nothing.

"Can I run you a shower? I'll stay with you the whole time."

"I'm never going to dance again," Gabe moans.

"Of course you are, darling."

Gabe lets his arm thud back to the ground, beating his fist against the carpet. "This is so fucking unfair. I'm a good dancer. I don't want to die weak."

Josie's expression splinters before he can right himself. "You're not going to die," Josie asserts thinly. "You're going to get through this."

"For how long?" Gabe heaves. "I'm ruining our lives."

"Gabe," says Josie, craning over Gabe, his palms flat on the floor on either side of Gabe's shoulders. "You aren't. Of *course* you aren't."

Gabe's face contorts, his mouth frozen in a little *o* of misery, eyes rolled into the back of his skull. There is something so plainly ugly about his show of agony, so alarmingly unlike himself.

"I know you think it!" Gabe explodes on the release of a sob, spittle foaming on his lower lip. "From the way you treat me!"

"Gabe, no," Josie says, his voice emerging in a strangulated squeak, "No! I really don't!"

"We don't even fuck anymore," Gabe laments.

Josie's cheeks flush, his lips pinched tight. It takes him a long moment to answer. "That's not true."

"Isn't it?" Gabe says. "Can you remember the last time you fucked me?"

Josie looks away. Gabe knows Josie can't remember; Gabe cannot either. And any of Josie's usual reasoning—*you need the little energy you have, I'm responsible for nursing you, it doesn't feel more important than you recovering*—is too damning to say aloud.

"You know I don't care about things like that," Josie objects. He blanches the moment the words are out of his mouth; it is an equally damning thing to admit.

Gabe plants his hand in the middle of Josie's chest and pushes away from him miserably. Gabe hears Josie thud back onto his backside.

"I want to sleep," Gabe bawls. "Leave me alone."

Josie sits on the floor beside him, breathing heavily. Gabe only stops crying once it becomes too painful to continue, a throbbing ice pick behind his left eye. After a long silence, Josie asks, "Can I take you to bed?"

Gabe doesn't reply, watching his own fist tighten and uncurl. It doesn't feel like his own hand, or his own body. He's an intruder in a foreign vessel. Talking feels beyond his ability.

In time, Josie lies down on the floor as well, just out of Gabe's line of vision.

SIX DAYS

Lisi is barred from the bedroom when Gabe's first seizure starts. She waits downstairs in the unsettling quiet for news from Josie.

In time, Josie emerges from upstairs, disheveled and wild-eyed.

"You can see him now," he says with a calmness that is alarmingly incongruent with his appearance.

"What can I do to help?" Lisi asks.

She is braced for Josie's firm rejection, but instead he says, "Why don't you bring him some water?"

It's less a suggestion than a demand, but Lisi is grateful for her inclusion.

So she brings him water in a small plastic cup and kneels beside the bed to help him drink, because his hands are too weak to clasp it. Then she cleans the excess that dribbles off his chin and the sloppy line of spittle that stretches from his lower lip to the glass. A part of her knows this disgusts her, but more presently, she doesn't want him to be embarrassed. She knows Gabe too well to let him sit undignified.

"Hi," says Gabe, blinking up at her erratically. She squeezes his shoulder in response. "Is Josie here?" he asks.

"I am," says Josie from the doorway.

"Oh, good," Gabe says. He giggles deliriously. "Here comes Josie. Josie will fix me."

His head slants stiffly toward Lisi until his temple collides hard against her shoulder. She winces, more for his sake than her own.

"Lisi," he says, in a voice that startles her. Low and resonant. A voice that truly sounds like Gabe. His posture rights, disentangling himself from the ungraceful slump against her body. "We'll have to leave for Sacramento tomorrow," Gabe says apologetically between thin, measured breaths.

"Oh, Gabe, I don't care," Lisi says and is walloped with the instantaneous realization that she means it. She can hardly recall how many days there are until Impact.

Gabe's brow knits together, his glassy eyes suddenly pricked with tears. "You're just a baby," he says. Just as quickly, Gabe's eyes roll into the back of his head, and his jaw snaps shut.

Josie hastily shoves her aside, fixing Gabe's pillows so that he can't injure himself as he thrashes. Lisi is winded, though it is hard to discern if it is from the force of Josie's impact, or the panic constricting her lungs.

Gabe tosses and jerks spasmodically in eerie silence.

"Aren't you supposed to hold them down?" Lisi asks. She is embarrassed by the sound of her own voice, weak and childish.

"That's only in movies, Lisi," says Josie gruffly.

Unwelcome and scared, she takes the plastic cup and goes.

Hours pass without word from Josie. The sun begins to slant back over the western hills, the light turning the outdoor pool a slick, undulating gold. It gives Lisi a seasick feeling she can't explain, the taste of bile at the back of her throat.

She returns upstairs, but the bedroom is empty, sheets left in disarray, pillows scattered on the floor. Unthinkingly, Lisi shouts for Josie.

The door to the en suite bathroom swings open, and Josie steps out. He has eked past disheveled, now sunken-eyed and haggard and, to Lisi's confusion, wet. His arms are still dripping, the entire front of his shirt nearly translucent.

"I. You. Didn't come get me," she explains haltingly, suddenly feeling like a child in trouble with their schoolteacher.

Instead of the snappish pragmatism she expects, Josie clucks and runs his wet hands through his hair. "Sorry. I've been busy. I forgot."

"It's okay," she says.

"What I mean is . . . I wasn't trying to. I didn't realize the time—" Josie stammers. He seems genuinely panicked by the notion, very much unlike the Josie she'd known as Gabe's even-keeled warden.

"It's okay," Lisi repeats, lifting her hands as if in supplication, absolving Josie of the guilt. "How is he?"

"The time between seizures is getting smaller. Which is not good. It means we never really stopped the first one."

"Oh," says Lisi. Conceptually, she understands what Josie is saying, but it feels so far away from her, merely the idea of sickness, just the kind of words people say on television. It won't be real until she can see him. It can't be real until she can see him.

She angles her body to squeeze past Josie in the doorway.

"Lisi, Lisi," Josie says, stopping her with a firm hand on her shoulder. She tries to push past but he is immovable. Lisi beats him in height, but Josie is grounded and strong as a workhorse, and just as intractably stubborn.

"Let me in."

"I put him in the bath," Josie explains apologetically.

"So?"

"So he's . . ." Josie hedges. "You know what I'm going to say. He's nude."

"So I won't look," she says, throwing her hands in the air. "I'm not a . . . a baby!"

Josie looks at her so pityingly that Lisi's stomach turns with disgust.

"Lisi, it's ugly. He's really . . . um." His voice tapers into a whisper. "Really not doing well. I've never seen it this bad."

"I know that," she bargains. "That's why I have to come in, Jo."

She realizes she has used Gabe's nickname for him before she can even doubt if it's appropriate, or why it came to her mind unbidden. She's never called him that before.

Josie seems equally struck by it—confused, but not alarmed. He exhales through his teeth and steps aside, letting Lisi past.

Josie has kept the room dim. The only light comes from two decorative candles, and the small bathroom smells not quite pleasantly of both cinnamon and white flowers. Gabe is laid out in the bathtub, his head pillowed by rolled towels. Lisi averts her eyes where expected, which is not difficult. His face catches her attention first.

The hot water does seem to have relaxed his tense muscles. His eyes are closed, but his jaw hangs open now, instead of clenched irontight. But in his pliancy, his bonelessness, he looks less like himself. His eyes seem sunken, his low, sharp cheekbones gaunt. Lisi touches her own face reflexively, feeling herself mirrored in the unusual planes of Gabe's angular face. But her own skin is warm and supple with good health.

Gabe does not respond to the disruption of their argument nor their entrance into the bathroom. Josie does not address him, so Lisi follows suit, keeping her voice low so as not to disturb what she hopes is merely a deep sleep.

"What do we do without his medication?" Lisi asks. She feels Josie shift uncomfortably behind her.

"If we can stop the seizures, if we can get that under control, I can maybe try and . . . try and find other medication to work as a stopgap."

"I thought you said we hadn't stopped the first seizure."

Josie doesn't respond to that. He gently pushes past Lisi and regains his post, kneeling by the bathtub. Lisi sits atop the toilet to allow room for them both.

"Gabe," he beckons gently. "We're both here for you. Will you open your eyes and look at us?"

"Can he hear you?" Lisi asks.

Josie ignores her, continuing to murmur pleasant nonsense over Gabe's body.

Gabe seizes again. The fit is shorter and less violent than what she'd witnessed before, but that discomforts her. His body seems utterly spent, exhausted beyond function. She recalls Gabe's heavy, bald head when she visited at Thanksgiving, swinging limply on his thin neck. It is so strange, so incongruous, to know Gabe is even sicker now. That, in the face of the worst of it, the grotesque images she replayed guiltily in her mind actually amounted to very little.

Josie fastidiously adjusts the towels around Gabe's neck and head. "Gabe," Josie speaks into his ear. He gently massages along his jaw, hoping to relax him, or even capture his attention. Gabe says nothing. The only sound is the rasp of his shallow breath.

Josie falls back heavily, spent, the sandbag of his wide torso colliding against the bathroom wall with a resonant thud.

"I can keep watch for a while," Lisi offers.

Josie doesn't respond. Though Lisi is in his line of sight, his eyes are vacant and dark.

"Really," she insists. "I'm right here. I promise I'll shout if I need you."

"I said something last night that really upset him," Josie mumbles. His arms hang limply at his sides, except for his hands which twitch and stretch like strange injured birds. "What if I set him off?"

"That . . ." Lisi stammers, flabbergasted, "that's a really mean thing to say to yourself."

"I don't know how to help him," he says. "I'm not a doctor. I can't stop the—the pain he's in."

Gabe's breath hitches. Lisi extends her hand timidly, as if Josie will spring to halt her, but Josie's blazing panic has burned down to embers. He is catatonic with the weight of defeat, seeing and hearing nothing.

Lisi feels a rare clarity. She touches Josie's shoulder, and then Gabe's forehead.

"Gabe," she says, loud enough to jostle Josie out of his stupor. "Gabe. We love you so much. It's okay."

Josie looks at her with a wild, accusatory panic.

"What are you doing," he warns, without the pretense of a question.

"It's okay, Gabe," she repeats, undeterred. "We love you so much. We're right here."

"Stop telling him that," Josie says. "It's not okay. Gabe. It's not okay."

Lisi resents the ending of the world—that she won't get to make more art or be famous, that she won't meet new friends. That a love like Gabe and Josie's was possible, but she'd never get to experience it. Lisi cannot make peace with that.

But she loves Gabe so thoroughly. So tremendously. All of those things she ached to achieve, anything worth reaching for and mourning the loss of, was because Gabe had told her she could. Lisi was Gabe's creation, the dedicated molding of his clay. And she was so proud to be Gabe's. Lisi and Josie; they were his. And that love would keep him bound to them for as long they persisted, hauling Gabe behind, scraping him down to nothing.

"You can let go, Gabe," she says. "We don't want you to be in pain."

Josie leans forward and grips her knee bruisingly hard. "*Stop*," he warns. "What if he hears you?"

"He does, Jo," she says. "He does. Look."

Gabe's contorted expression has softened, his breathing shallow but even. Lisi can't tell if she's imagined it—a sort of wishful thinking—but his face seems to be angled up toward the sound of their voices.

"We love you so much, Gabe," she says. "We're not scared."

Josie's anger has petered into bald desperation. He clasps his arms tight around Lisi's knees, his face in her lap. It is so wretched, so unlike him, that she nearly buckles. Gabe had warned her: Josie would need them at the end. "I'm begging you," Josie whines. "I'm begging you to stop."

"Gabe, do you remember when you tried to bleach your hair? Do you remember you wanted to do it at my house? You must've known it was going to destroy all the towels and your parents would've killed you." Lisi chuckles and cups Gabe's cool cheek. "God, it looked awful. And you could pull anything off." She pinches his earlobe affectionately. "You were the only trouble worth getting in."

She looks down at Josie expectantly. He disentangles himself from around her knees, a flash of shame twisting his expression. Lisi's instinct was correct. Gabe has slackened. Whether a peacefulness has overtaken him or merely exhaustion, neither of them could know for certain. But his brow is no longer lined with tension, his sloped shoulders heavy and loose.

"You came to the ceremony for my master's degree," Josie says, his voice crackling in and out like the weak-signaled radio broadcasts they listened to each morning. "We'd only been dating for a few weeks, but you really wanted to come."

Lisi watches how Josie succumbs to the memory, how even with his hands fisted, white-knuckled, in his jeans, his expression softens. His lips twist upward into a smile. *There's the Josie that Gabe loves*, she thinks. *Didn't he deserve to be here?*

"I would've never said so," Josie continues, "but I was so jealous of everyone with family there. So jealous and so sad. But then there was you." He reaches into the water and takes Gabe's limp hand. "You brought—oh, the *mess*. You brought so many bouquets and big balloons that they were confiscated at the door."

Lisi erupts with laughter, and Josie can't help but follow. "Is that true?"

"Yes," Josie giggles wetly. "They said it was disruptive. They took it all to the trash. But Gabe wouldn't leave until he got it all back."

Lisi reflexively looks to Gabe for his reaction, eternally eager to follow his lead. The impulse is foolish, almost maudlin, but it doesn't fluster her. It feels appropriate to include him in their laughter.

"You must have been embarrassed," she tells him.

But it is Josie who responds, chewing his lips thoughtfully before concluding, "I should've been. But he didn't let me."

"Different rules apply in Gabe's world," Lisi proclaims.

Josie looks up at her and seems to sincerely regard not only that silly quip, but Lisi herself. He is looking right at her now, in her eyes. "Yes," he says.

She nods at him. He nods back.

His sweet, round face then crumples, mangled in an eerie, elongated moment of silent anguish. Lisi fears he may erupt into hysterics. But instead he exhales, and as he does he leans forward, his arm plunging into the bathtub up past the sleeve of his shirt. He cups his other hand around the back of Gabe's neck and kisses Gabe's limp lower lip.

"It's okay if you have to go," he mumbles against his slack mouth. "I love you. Thank you. Thank you."

He remains hunched over Gabe, his arms submerged, clasping Gabe against him. After each infrequent breath—a long, slow hiss like a radiator—Josie kisses him. Gabe's rattling chest becomes alarmingly loud, and then alarmingly quiet.

Josie's arms begin to tremble, weakened by the weight they're holding. It is then that Lisi realizes the moment has passed—the electric, kinetic bundle of strong muscles under Gabe's skin has now gone fully slack, Josie cleaving to an expression Lisi'd never fully considered before: dead weight.

"Jo," Lisi says quietly.

"Stop," Josie rasps. "I know."

Lisi rests her palm on the top of Josie's head. There is a sharp inhale, and then Josie yowls, completely without tears, until his voice gives out.

Morning arrives quickly. Lisi spots the sunrise first through the small bathroom window. At some juncture, Josie had slumped against the wall and remained there, catatonic and mute. She is loath to disturb him, frightened of what wild wheel of grief might froth out of him next.

Instead, it is Josie who first takes note of the time.

"'S morning already," he slurs, jutting his chin sluggishly toward the window.

Lisi studies him: his impassive face, lined with exhaustion, his cloudy eyes and gray lips. "Josie, will you eat?"

"No thank you, Lisi," he says. "Let's get to Sacramento."

"Oh," says Lisi, her voice splintering glass. "What does it matter?"

Josie rises to his feet and claps his hand on her shoulder. "Let's go," he announces. "I don't want to be here anymore."

Josie withdraws in a way that Lisi recognizes. He parses out life in manageable tasks and looks no further than the next one. He drains the bathtub of the cold water, but not before using the last few handfuls to scrub Gabe's sallow face clean with a cotton washcloth. Gabe's chapped lower lip momentarily catches on the cloth and it is tugged forward, distorting his expression. There is such a strange indignity in it, something so dopey and unguarded and nearly alive, that Lisi finds herself repulsed and has to look away. By the time she looks back, Josie has covered Gabe with a bath towel. It was the last glimpse she'd ever have of his face, and she'd squandered it. But she could not admit that to Josie, least of all herself, so the both of them dutifully move on.

They close the door to the bathroom. They make all the beds. They collect their clothes and food and bags. Josie teeters on the brink of utter collapse, but Lisi knows he won't plummet over the edge. He is far too good, too practiced, in the face of devastation. Josie has experienced the end of the world over and over again, to varying degrees, for years.

Lisi doesn't ask permission to drive, she merely takes up the position. Josie rides beside her in silence, with Gabe's small bag of belongings clutched in his lap. Lisi insists he eat at some point, and at another instance they pull over to stretch their legs on the side of the California state highway, but the day occurs in snapshots, and Josie only hazily recollects the joining moments. He feels brittle in his exhaustion, too weary to even feel the dread of the waning days, though it still ticks like the hammer of an alarm bell in the back of his mind.

"Do you see how light it is?" Lisi asks, peering up through the dusty windshield.

Josie is startled by the sound of her voice, which in her low, melodic timbre had almost sounded more like the start of a song eking through the sporadic radio signal.

"Hm?"

"The sky. Look," Lisi urges.

The bright bulb of the sun has sunk beneath the horizon, but the sky is still glowing, striated with breathtaking color that reminds Josie of the Grand Canyon. It should be beautiful. Instead, it pangs him with a constricting panic knowing the Intruder is up there, approaching but beyond his sight.

The clock on the dashboard reads 9:10 p.m.

Lisi laughs through her unease. "It's kinda fucking with my eyes."

"Oh," Josie says, his tongue heavy in his mouth, feeling like a machine clicking back into operation. "Let me drive."

"No, no," Lisi is quick to answer. "I don't want you to. I think we both should rest. Don't you?"

Her expression is uncertain and eager. If Josie is being tricked into being coddled, he is too exhausted to mind.

Josie shifts onto his side, his cheek pressing into the body-warmed leather of the car seat. "I could close my eyes for a bit," he admits. He inhales shakily. "Pretty tired."

There are no trees to pull beneath to hide the car anymore. He vaguely recalls Lisi mentioning something about the Mojave Desert region, back when they were still panicked about their dwindling gas tank. Lisi drives until the metal highway dividers disappear and cautiously pulls over onto a dusty bit of land flanked by a stubby plateau of rock. It provides the slightest charade of some safety and privacy.

It's oppressively quiet. There isn't even the familiar ocean-tide whoosh of passing cars. Far as they are from any humanity, the world should be dark around them, but instead the sky remains a bright, eerie pink. Josie still instinctively turns on the overhead light in the car while they prepare themselves for sleep.

"Your eye looks a lot better," Lisi says. Josie is startled, already half-lost to unconsciousness. She angles in her seat to lay facing him. "The bruise is basically gone."

"It feels fine," Josie answers. The air between them feels magnetized; he can sense her preparing to say something else.

"Do you believe in past lives?"

"No," says Josie flatly.

"Do you know what I think you were?" She pauses. "Sorry, do you hate this?"

"I don't hate it, Lisi," he answers, eyes still closed. "What was I?"

"I think you might have been a cowboy. Or a pioneer, something like that. Some survivalist who packed up and risked it all to find a life that suited him."

"Hm," says Josie sleepily.

"You have a spirit of forward motion."

Josie smiles at that. He repeats it back to her thoughtfully, appreciatively: a spirit of forward motion. It resonates with him, for whatever reason.

"I could see you on a horse," she muses, which makes Josie sputter a small laugh, more exhalation than sound.

"I like horses," he says.

Lisi turns off the overhead bulb and Josie drifts off to sleep, curled up in the passenger's seat, listening to Lisi laughingly recall some gauche play she'd seen about gay frontiersmen. He regrets never having seen one of Lisi's performances. He quite likes the sound of her voice.

FOUR DAYS

They wake with the sun, which shines bright and unrelenting off the copper dirt and the yellow plane of stone behind them. Lisi encourages Josie to stretch for a bit and tries to make food sound tempting. But once they are out of the car, they can feel that the air has changed. It is heavy and smells sweet, like ozone. Dead birds litter the roadsides.

Josie regards the scene, frozen and wild-eyed, with the quality of a spooked horse. "Four days," he says.

Lisi points to a road sign along the highway. "Fresno. I've been here before. We're like, three hours from Sacramento."

"Easy trip," says Josie.

"Easy trip," Lisi echoes, completely devoid of sarcasm, which makes Josie titter a delirious little laugh.

The trip is as uncomplicated as they'd hoped. The highways are empty, and Josie allows himself to speed, absorbing some of Lisi's palpable anticipation. They pull up at her front door just after ten.

Josie had always known Lisi had money but is still taken aback by the sheer loveliness of her house. The front lawn is overgrown but lush and green. The paint is white and fresh. The shiny limestone walkway reminds Josie of the inside of a museum.

Lisi darts out of the car. It fills Josie with a happiness he sincerely did not think he would feel upon arriving—not just a sense of accomplishment for making the journey, but a genuine thrill at seeing Lisi's relief, the childish way she sprints up the walkway without even closing the car door behind her.

He collects her bag and follows, stepping through the open front door. The interior is just as well-appointed—clean and chic and white. He cranes his head up the gently curved staircase, adorned with professionally taken photos.

He hears Lisi calling for her parents in the kitchen. She speeds by Josie, circling the foyer, the living room, the patio.

"Did they step out?" Josie suggests, as she tears up the stairs still shouting for their attention.

Josie follows slowly behind her, suddenly feeling like a man climbing to the gallows.

He's at her heels when she finds them in their bedroom, both face-down on the cream-colored carpet. Strewn about them are pills, dotted between their splayed fingers, scattering outward from an upturned empty bottle.

Josie reels at the scene—the ugly shock of it all—but chiefly at the smell, which is unlike anything he has ever experienced. They were dead, and it had not been recent.

Lisi screams and distantly Josie thinks he's never heard anything like it before. It's inhuman. It's repulsive. He doesn't mean to, but he recoils.

Lisi's knees hit the floor. She rocks uneasily there, then pitches forward head-first, already unconscious before she hits the ground.

THREE DAYS

Lisi blinks awake, a splitting pain between her eyes. She knows she should muster some small amount of fear—waking in an unknown place, after an unknown stretch of time, sore and heavy all over—but she feels nothing. There's a pillow under her head that smells familiar. The sheets are soft and worn. An old Annie Lennox poster is plastered to the wall above her head, the corners curling out of their scotch tape with age, and above the open door, there's a banner of colorful felt letters strung together spelling out LISETTE. She is in her childhood bedroom, in her bed.

The memory of her last conscious thoughts rush her like a riptide. She bites the inside of her cheek to stifle a sob that bubbles up her throat.

"Josie?" she calls into the silence, rising up on her unsteady forearms. She hears his heavy footsteps tearing up the stairs and toward her bedroom.

Josie skids to a stop in the open doorway. "You're awake," he says. "I was worried about you."

"How did I get here?"

"I—" Josie begins, then halts. Lisi watches him scan her face, and then the room around her, before casting a brief glance over his shoulder.

"Do you mean your house?" he asks, lowly. "How much do you remember?"

"I remember," she snaps, a bit more acidly than she'd intended. She could not bear to hear the events summarized in Josie's sober, plain-spoken way. It would unravel her. "How did I get to my bed?"

Josie focuses on Lisi's armoire on the other side of the room, a ruddy blush mottling his neck. "I took you here," he says.

"You *carried* me to bed?"

Josie lifts his shoulders in a half-aborted shrug. "I couldn't leave you there."

"Gentleman, you are," Lisi grunts, casting her humor out like a lifeboat, something the two of them might cleave to for some needed normalcy. But the gibe lands flatly between them. She manages to right herself, feeling suddenly vulnerable with all of her reactions so carefully monitored.

"Thank you for doing that." Lisi says. Josie nods stiffly. "How long have I been out?"

"Um, a while," Josie hedges. "Don't freak out."

"I'm not freaking out," she says, certain that she is. She shoves her shaking hands beneath her thighs.

"It's tomorrow," Josie answers. "I mean, it's been since yesterday. You slept all night."

Lisi tries to process this. Now there are only three days left, or maybe two. It's gotten increasingly difficult to keep track.

"Where are they?"

"What?"

"My—" Lisi begins but stops herself, her eyes rolling into the back of her head. She nods twice, sharply, as if willing herself back to consciousness. "The bodies."

"I took them outside," Josie explains. "Is that bad?"

"Why?"

"I . . ." says Josie, looking contrite, "I didn't think you should see them."

Lisi's kneejerk instinct is to resist. She resents being coddled after all this time together and has always despised being told what to do. After all, it was her house and her parents. Bile quickly rises and burns her throat.

"Fine," she says instead. "You're probably right."

She brushes the hair out of her face and winces, a sharp pain blossoming at her temple, just above her left eyebrow.

"Oh no no no," Josie gasps, abandoning the chivalry of not entering without invitation. He rushes to her bedside. "You hit your head yesterday when you, um . . ." He pauses. ". . . fell."

"It fucking hurts," Lisi moans.

Josie carefully lifts the curtain of her bangs to inspect her. After a long and cautious moment, he must deem the wound acceptable—or at least not worse—and says, "Do you want food? I managed to find some nonperishables."

Josie helps her out of bed gingerly. She tries to walk ahead of him but crumples against the railing the moment she takes the first stair. Her knees seem unwilling to lock into place. Josie's arm is at her waist in an instant. She leans heavily against his side as they wind down the staircase in silence.

Josie's well of patience seems unending, his desire to help inextinguishable. It is, at the basest level, why Lisi had felt estranged from him for so long. Josie's uncomplicated integrity made Lisi feel small in its presence. She could not discern whether selflessness like his was practiced, or cultivated, or inherent from birth. And in trying to parse it, she only felt further from—in her spiteful imagination—the hot and human wellspring of goodness. Always standing apart from it, resentful and lacking.

She regrets so much of the time she hated Josie, when it was never that Josie was good. It was that Lisi couldn't comprehend why she wasn't.

"This is insane," Lisi grouses. "I should be taking care of you."

"Hush," says Josie. It reminds Lisi of a stern old schoolteacher. He deposits her neatly in one of the high chairs at the kitchen counter and slides a bowl in front of her.

Josie has strained the chicken and the noodles out of a can of Campbell's and laid it atop a bowl of mixed beans. Lisi looks at him quizzically.

"You didn't just heat up the soup?"

"No power," says Josie, gesturing vaguely toward the ceiling. "No gas."

"Oh," Lisi answers, and the image of Josie sitting awake all the last evening, in the absolute darkness without company or distraction, shoots her through like a spear.

"But look," Josie says, pulling something onto the counter. It is a dusty radio, about the size of Josie's hand. "Battery powered, so it still works. Your parents were smart."

Lisi must recoil at the mention of her parents in an alarming way, because Josie apologizes and falls into an uneasy silence as Lisi eats. The food is better than she expected.

"I can leave you alone," Josie says, just as Lisi timidly ventures,

"Maybe I can show you around?"

Lisi is good at telling stories, though Josie is only half-attentive, shuffling behind Lisi as she begins her unfocused but sincere tour around her home. He is very conscious of the fact that she bypasses her parents' bedroom with her eyes lowered, and neither parent appears in any of the memories she recounts.

Josie had heard people claim that returning to a childhood home reverts a person into a younger, arrested version of themselves. He would never experience this. He had never gone back home. He feels, in some ways, that he'd never been a child.

When Lisi stops Josie to eagerly show him a certificate she'd been granted in high school for winning a state-wide monologue competition, it almost makes his teeth ache, to think of her so young and so proud of herself—still young, and still proud of herself, and looking to Josie for the approval Gabe used to supply in spades. An approval Josie had denied her for so long.

She was selfish. She was disorganized. She was repulsed by hardship. So many people her age were. So many people Josie's age were too. But none of those facts ever absolved her of her shortcomings, because behaving that way simply didn't make sense to Josie. Overlaid against Lisi was, and eternally would be, the girls Josie did not finish raising and all the imagined ways they would exceed Lisi, had he not run away fifteen years ago.

They meander into the living room. Josie appreciates how nicely appointed it is: the picture frames, the modern lamps, the matching white couches. He nearly laughs imagining his own family home with a stark-white couch, and how quickly it would've been ruined beyond recognition.

Lisi has busied herself at one of the bookcases, digging around until she procures what she's looking for with a triumphant grunt.

"This is the one," Lisi says, and motions for Josie to come closer.

"What's that?"

"Pictures. Do you want to see?"

He nods, and Lisi gestures broadly for him to make himself comfortable. He looks at the white couches and chooses instead to sit on the floor. Lisi settles beside him, turning thoughtfully from page to page. He cranes over her shoulder eagerly.

"I know it's in this one somewhere," she ruminates under her breath, flipping to the next page.

"There you are," says Josie, stilling her hand before she can turn again. He points to a photo of a group of people sitting on the floor around an ornate Christmas tree, little Lisi in the middle. She is young, and without her stylish haircut or clothes, but still instantly recognizable, long-limbed and dark-eyed behind a curtain of her pin-straight long hair.

"My parents got me a kitten that Christmas," Lisi says. "From a friend of theirs in the neighborhood."

"Mm," says Josie, more interested in Lisi's young beaming face, searching for traces of Gabe in her smile.

"But the kitten was sick, which they didn't know. He just didn't eat, or drink, or anything. It was pretty clear it was going to die. I think a lot of kittens do. And this one was just not going to get better with, you know, medicine. I remember that I understood that."

He watches Lisi's fingers wind tight into the hair behind her right ear, the same as when he'd found her panicking in Las Vegas. Her hand tenses, flexes, and then falls limply back into her lap, as if responding to chastisement Josie cannot hear.

"So they took the kitten back to their friend. And I remember asking them why. I knew it was going to die. So if it's going to die anyway, why does it have to go somewhere else to do it? He was mine." Lisi's throat pinches closed on the last word, pitching her voice high like the squeak of a balloon. "I don't know why I started telling that story," she intones, devoid of the usual musicality of her pattern of speech.

Josie rests his hand on her shoulder, and then the back of her neck, as if she were a spooked animal. Her throat bobs as she manages one sharp, dry swallow.

"Lisi," he begins, but she has regained her momentum, and shrugs away from his touch.

"Wait. That isn't what I was trying to show you."

She hunches back over the book of photographs, undeterred this time. It takes a few moments, scanning each page, but with a triumphant gasp she pushes it toward Josie. "It's Gabe," she says. Josie's eyes well with tears at even the mention of his name. "I'm sorry. Should I not show you?"

Josie extends his hand to take it. "No, I want to see it. Please."

She passes over the book of photos with incredible care. Josie receives it, cradling it in the crook of his arm like it's a child. He angles away from her a bit, greedy for a moment of privacy with these precious, unexpected artifacts.

In the first photo, Gabe stands in the kind of dim, unremarkable, tan-bricked hallway one only finds in schools or community centers. He appears to be in his early teen years, no more than fourteen or fifteen, with a shock of thick black hair pushed away from his forehead with so much hair gel that the dome of his head shines in the light as if it were plastic. The costume he wears is both gaudy and silly—a tight brocade jacket and opaque white tights. Nonetheless, he is beaming, with an arm full of yellow and white flowers and a fair amount of blush on his cheeks. He is poised—posed, even—his feet in fifth position and his shoulders pushed back.

In the second photo, taken perhaps only moments later, Lisi is entwined around Gabe, a grin of unbridled joy on her prepubescent face.

There are only two photographs, but Josie pores over them with immeasurable delight. The sadness is a pinprick against the pleasure, the gratification he feels in being able to see Gabe once more. A Gabe he'd never known and would never know: spry, gawky, a mouth full of silver braces, and an outdated haircut.

"I remember it was right after Christmas," Lisi explains. "*The Nutcracker*. He had a big role even though it was his first season with the studio! It was the first time I saw him dance."

"Thank you for showing this to me, Lisi," Josie says as he hands back the book. "Look how happy you are."

Lisi, too, lingers on the photos as they return to her care.

"I'm squeezing the shit out of him," she chuckles. "I was totally starstruck."

Josie understands that sentiment well.

Lisi's eyes narrow, her mouth falling open. "He dyed his shoes," she says, with a gasp of delight. "Yes!" The momentum of the memory piecing itself back together quickens Lisi's tempo. "He was the only person on stage with navy blue shoes . . . and we asked! We were like, 'Why did every other boy have those white canvas shoes?' And he was so casual about it, like it was so obvious, like, 'Oh, these are the same shoes, I just hated that they didn't match my jacket—so I dyed them.' Because he was playing some kind of prince or something?"

She's reaching toward Josie, palm outstretched, as if he might be able to supplement the details of the memory with his own, as if he were there, as if he'd always been part of their lives.

"And his toes were blue after that for *weeks*!"

Lisi and Josie traverse the same arc of thought, immediately, and with revulsion. Lisi snaps the book of photos closed.

"Josie?" she asks thinly, tremulously, like a person about to confess their guilt. "Should we have buried Gabe? I'm afraid."

"Of what?" says Josie.

"I don't know. It's so stupid. I don't even believe in it. But . . ." She turns and faces Josie, summoning her resolve. "Like, in your religion—how you were raised, or whatever it is you still believe—are there rules like that? Did we do the right thing for Gabe, in case?"

"In case of what?"

"In case of an *after*."

Josie did not want to think about an after. The notion still terrified him, and neither time nor distance from his childhood could assuage the cold grip of dread. Josie had long ago resolved to be different. New York made that easy: no one seemed to care where he grew up, or if he spent all of his holidays working; and if his life was lonely, it was nothing more than a drop in the bracing, ice-cold, wonderful ocean that was his freedom. When old impulses wrenched their way to the surface—chiefly, when God came to mind—it was always unwillingly and reflexively. An act of self-excoriation.

"I guess we'd bury someone in a casket after a funeral," Josie says, grasping at rationality. "But you don't have to. There's not a rule."

"And you'd say a prayer for them?"

"I suppose."

"I want us to do that," Lisi insists, wagging her index finger enthusiastically in Josie's direction. "Can you tell me what to say?"

"To *say*?" Josie splutters. "It doesn't matter. You just talk, Lisi."

"To God?"

Josie fights the instinct to throw up his hands in frustration. "If that's what makes you happy," he says.

"I just want to do what's right," she protests anemically. Her restless hands wind around and around each other in her lap, her eyes flicking from the carpet, to Josie, then back to the carpet.

It is still a shock to witness Lisi in moments of speechlessness, of deep abashment. But Josie figures he can't curb her resolve, only embarrass her further, so he racks his brain for some pleasant-sounding text that doesn't evoke anything too religious.

He nods at Lisi, who obediently rises to her knees, clasping her hands before her. She looks more like a handsome actor on stage aping at penance, with her wide mournful eyes cast heavenward. But she says nothing and waits eagerly for Josie to begin. He refuses to kneel and instead sits cross-legged facing her. He clears tightness from his throat.

"Eternal rest grant unto Gabe," he says. Each word feels as if it has been scraped, with monumental effort, out from treacherous, cavernous places inside himself, where his discomfort coalesced with his grief.

"We come before you with all the sorrow and pain that is in our hearts today. May the words of our mouths and the meditations of our hearts be acceptable in your sight."

Lisi nods along with him. "And whatever happens to us all," she continues, taking up the mantle, "let good things come to Gabe. We did what we could in the, um, the given circumstances." Josie notes how she winces at her own words, aware of the lack of poetry, of the pedestrian, almost arbitration-like nature of it all. "And I'm sorry I wasn't better to Gabe when he needed it. I didn't know how to be better. It was all so scary. He looked so sick."

Josie nods along with her, trying hard not to let any of the imagery Lisi so clearly is revisiting in her own mind swim unbidden into his.

"But I didn't try," she says. "I left him. I think about that night all the time. You know that. Don't you?"

Josie looks askance at Lisi, who no longer casts her eyes upward but speaks directly to Josie. Her eyes are bright and heavy with unshed tears.

"Which night? Was I there?"

"Of course you were," Lisi warbles. "You know what I'm talking about."

The realization settles over Josie like heavy silt. He can hardly move under the weight. "Yes," he says.

"You know I never forgave myself, right? You know that? It was the . . . the worst thing I've ever—"

"Oh, Lisi," he exhales. "I think Gabe was so out of it, he probably didn't even realize."

"But *you* knew," she insists. "You must have hated me."

"I never hated you," says Josie, and this, he realizes with certainty, is true. He resented her freedom. He resented her choices. He resented her connection to a family that could have improved the quality of Gabe's life with their money and affection, but for reasons obscured to Josie, would not. But Lisi he did not hate, even at her most cowardly and vain, because what they had in common was an immutable love of the same person.

"You've always been good to me," Lisi says with a wet hiccup. She shuffles gawkily on her knees to close the short distance between them and threads her arms around Josie.

"I hate them," she chokes. "Why didn't they wait for me? They knew we were coming."

Josie feels the pat of warm tears upon his shoulder. "They must have been scared, Lisi," he says, his hands alighting on her ribcage.

He hadn't realized how slight and bony she would feel. How much it recalled Gabe in his sickness. "Aren't you scared?"

"You would have waited. If it were Gabe trying to come home to you. You would have waited for him."

Josie wants to protest that he doesn't know what he would do. It was all so massive, so unimaginable. But Lisi had witnessed everything: the loss, and the journey, and the sickness, back to the earliest days of their relationship.

Yes, he would have waited for Gabe. Who else in his life did he have to live and wait for?

"No one has ever loved me like that," she wails, squeezing Josie harder.

He has no idea what to say. His heart breaks with hers, holding her there on the floor of the house she grew up in, bereft of the homecoming she imagined.

The crackle of the radio wakes them. They had succumbed to a motionless, fatigued sleep on the floor of the living room, hollowed out from so much emotion. Lisi is roused first and rises to peer out at a bright, gray morning. She'd slept pillowed against Josie's bicep all night, his palm cupped protectively against the back of her head. His sweetness still surprised her and filled her with homesickness.

"You okay?" Josie rasps. He stretches his arms above his head stiffly, blinking up at her with heavy, swollen eyes.

"The radio started up," Lisi says as she pulls it near. Josie rises to his knees, hovering close.

"Increasingly alarming data . . ." it says, spluttering in and out of service. Josie fiddles cautiously with the antenna. ". . . calculations have been checked and deemed accurate. We repeat: contrary to previous estimations, Impact will not be made tomorrow. We anticipate Impact will be reached in six to eight hours."

Lisi grips Josie's arm hard enough to bruise.

"God bless us all," the radio concludes, and clicks back into silence.

Josie carefully stands and reaches his arms wide. His eyes roll to the back of his head, sucking in a long, slow breath through his teeth, which he holds for a very, very long time.

"Jo?" she asks, reaching up to touch his hip. "Are you okay?"

He exhales violently, the sound like the firm sweep of a broom. His arms fall heavily back to his hips. He looks toward Lisi, and then the door.

"Do you know where my shoes are?"

They walk around the abandoned neighborhood together. Josie is quiet, so Lisi points out monuments of note: neighbors' homes that once housed old friends, trees where injuries were amassed, wooded dead-ends that served as the stages for Lisi and Gabe's one-person performances. It is unnaturally hot, and the emptiness of the world around them is disquieting, so they return home.

Lisi ambles around her childhood bedroom for a while, picking at old notebooks and memorabilia, eager to find something meaningful to present Josie with. The pursuit is quickly abandoned; everything fills her with a nauseous dissatisfaction.

She finds Josie in the kitchen, standing with his head bent, as if in prayer or deep thought, until Lisi realizes he is thoughtfully turning the half-empty bottle of sleeping pills over in his hand.

"Josie!" she reflexively admonishes and is instantly embarrassed by the naked terror in her voice.

The pills tumble from Josie's startled hands, and he snaps to her, stiff as a rod. "I wasn't!" Josie protests. "I promise. I was just looking."

"Looking for what?"

Josie's brow furrows, his plump lower lip hanging heavy. For the briefest moment, Lisi fears he's already taken the pills, suddenly listing into unconsciousness.

"There's quite a few left," he says, righting himself, very much awake.

"No," Lisi answers. And, at Josie's pitying look, shouts, "No!"

"It would just feel like sleeping," Josie says, but there's a desperation in his voice. The barest shade of a plea. "We don't know what will happen to us. We don't know if it will hurt."

"I can't stop you," says Lisi. "But I won't." She rolls her shoulders, peering out the window at an unnervingly light evening sky. "I won't. It disgusts me."

Lisi saw how Josie had handled Gabe's body. How fastidiously he'd cleaned and wrapped him, how that simple care felt like reverence. There was proof of their long, brilliant love in everything Josie did. There was a particular indignity Lisi felt but could not accurately express. Her parents were just bodies when she'd found them, bodies that Josie had to move out of pity, as if they were animals. She would be awake when it happened. She would not be vacant.

Josie's hand is on her back, gentle, like an apology. His skin is warm and grounding. "I want to go with you," Josie assures her. "Together."

They meander, distracted and unsettled, circling each other like dogs in a pen. Unable to sit, unable to communicate, but unwilling to wander too far. Josie stays occupied in the kitchen while Lisi paces the living room, gathering up the courage to look out of the window. The color of the sky has shifted to a sickly gray-green, the color of clouds before a summer storm, but unnervingly translucent. The sky seems low and puncturable, as if it were a ceiling of fog.

Lisi feels it first. A shortness of breath. A crackling in the air. The atmosphere has changed; perhaps siphoned off by the Intruder. It's close.

"Jo," she says, and he appears, wild-eyed, in the doorway.

"It's happening," he says, and Lisi nods. He stumbles toward her. "It's happening now."

Lisi swallows the stone in her throat. *Take care of Josie*, she recalls, very clearly. *I know it seems like he has it all together . . .*

"Where would you like to do this?" Lisi asks measuredly. She rolls her shoulders and tries to keep panic out of her expression so as not to startle Josie but realizes there's very little emotion to battle back. There's a cool sense of preparedness.

"I," says Josie, looking around at the unfriendly living room, the bright white couches, the house that was no homecoming. "I, um. I. Do you feel the, the, the air? It's so hard to breathe." He sways uneasily on his feet, a limp hand pressed against his throat. "I think I need to . . . sit down . . ."

"Here, Jo," says Lisi, helping him to the floor. Josie crumples uneasily onto his side, staring ahead unblinkingly. Lisi chooses to lie with him, face to face. He clings to her arm fiercely.

"Thank you, Lisi. Thank you."

"Of course," she says. She watches Josie's nostrils flare like a spooked horse. It is becoming increasingly hard to breathe. But all she can feel is pity.

"I'm sorry," Lisi erupts.

"For what?"

"I wish I were Gabe," she says. "I'm sorry he's not here."

That penetrates Josie, yanking him out of the grasp of morbidity. He emerges gasping Lisi's name. "Oh, Lisi. Don't say that. I love you."

"Do I look like him?" Lisi asks. "I've always thought he was so handsome."

He pushes the bangs back off Lisi's forehead. "Yes, you do," he says. "You have the same eyes and nose."

Lisi smiles. It's nice to know that, for whatever it's worth.

"Your poor forehead," Josie laments, which Lisi can't help but find vaguely hysterical. The wound is so small and insignificant. It all is. It all will be.

Josie touches her quivering lip. "Lisi?"

"Gabe really was my favorite person," she says.

"I know," Josie says, and Lisi believes he does.

"My parents didn't wait to see me."

"I know, Lisi. I'm so sorry."

The sound kicks up. First it's the pictures on the wall and the plates in the cabinets clinking and rattling about. Then a swelling rumble like that of a passing train.

"Josie?" she asks. The thin atmosphere feels sharp in her throat. "You really love me? Not like how you loved Gabe."

"I do," says Josie. "Not like how I loved Gabe. But I love you."

"Okay," she says. It bolsters her to hear that; puts steel in her spine. "I wanted to die with people who loved me."

The light now is unignorable. It doesn't feel anything like daylight. It's both blinding and devoid of any discernible color. Josie's eyes roll back, bleating a deep, low groan.

"I love you, Josie," she says. She brushes her fingers along his wet cheek, his hair, the hollow at the nape of his neck, just as Gabe had comforted her in this very room so many times.

Josie sees Gabe, illuminated, dark hair wet with sweat and plastered to his forehead, his white shirt semi-transparent in the stage lights. Gabe rising sharply out of a deep bow. *We have reached the end of our show*, Gabe says into the darkness, one hand raised as if in benediction. *Goodnight. See you when I see you.*

Josie doesn't know if he will. He wishes he believed in that or anything at all. The carpet beneath his cheek begins to vibrate.

"Oh god," Josie gasps. "Lisi. I'm scared. I'm really scared."

Lisi, for perhaps the first time in her life, feels an absolute sense of calm. Her purpose is singular and simple. It is all for Josie. It is exactly what she promised.

She pulls Josie close to her chest, lays her hand gently over Josie's eyes, and tells him to keep them closed. All at once, there is too much to make sense of. There's a roaring sound like a jet engine followed by a hot, white light. Josie trembles and sobs in her arms. Lisi presses a kiss to his brow, urges him to keep his eyes closed. It feels easy and familiar, as if she had done this before, as if it were inevitable. She tucks Josie beneath her chin so that he'll hear her.

It's not going to be much longer, Lisi tells him. She's with him at the end.

Acknowledgments

With deep gratitude to Mart Lett for the cover art, my family
and friends for their committed support (especially Marty and
Westley), my wonderful and extremely dead parents,
and the passionate members of Wildling Press.

ALI GORDON is a writer, performer, and educator living in Los Angeles. A New York City native, Ali spent many years in New York working as a musical theater actor as well as performing comedy at the renowned Upright Citizens Brigade theater. She holds a double major in musical theater and English from the University of Michigan. Ali also writes musicals and has performed and taught comedy all over the world. She promises she is quite funny despite the subject matter of this, her debut novel.

www.ingramcontent.com/pod-product-compliance
Lightning Source LLC
Chambersburg PA
CBHW021715190726
48289CB00008B/2539